The INITIATE

IN THE NEW WORLD

The INITIATE
IN THE NEW WORLD

Cyril Scott

SAMUEL WEISER, INC.
York Beach, Maine

This edition published in 1991 by
Samuel Weiser, Inc.
Box 612
York Beach, Maine 03910

First published in 1927 by
Routledge & Kegan Paul Ltd.
First paperback edition 1977

Library of Congress Cataloging in Publication Data

Scott, Cyril, 1879-1970
    The initiate in the new world: a sequel to "The initiate"/by
his pupil.—1st pbk. ed.
    p. cm.
    Reprint. Originally published: London: Routledge & Kegan
Paul, 1927
    1. Haig, Justin Moreward. 2. Spiritual life. 3. Occultists.
4. Gurus. I. Title.
BF1408.2.H35S35 1977   90-23038
133'.092—dc20   CIP

ISBN 0-87728-363-X
BJ

Cover art entitled "Time Travelers,"
©Rob Schouten, 1988. Used by kind permission of the artist.

Printed in the United States of America

CONTENTS

CONTENTS

INTRODUCTION

THE reception accorded to *The Initiate* has been at
once gratifying, instructive and curious. No less
than three different people have claimed to be its
author, and confided this intelligence to one of my
friends "in the know" who, with considerable amusement, passed it on to me without, I may add,
divulging their names; neither did he inform them of
the identity of the real author. The dishonesty of
these claimants is not without its element of flattery,
and they need not fear that, by way of retaliation,
I shall betray them by ceasing to preserve my
anonymity in this second *Initiate* book I am about
to send on its hazardous career. On the contrary,
I am grateful to them for thus assisting me to
maintain my literary disguise.

But apart from engendering this amusing species
of dishonesty, *The Initiate* has been responsible for
results less curious and more gratifying, if, at the
same time productive of certain embarrassments for
its author. For I have received, via my publishers,
letters in which the writers ask me either for "the
favour of an interview," or to obtain messages for

viii INTRODUCTION

them from my Master. In some cases they have
even specified what sort of message they want or do
not want, several having declared that they would by
no means be satisfied with advice or admonitions of
a "goody-goody" nature. Some of these correspondents I have replied to as best I could, others I
have deemed it wise to treat with silence knowing
that one day they will come to learn that Masters
cannot be dictated to in the manner implied, and that
the only message a Master could be expected to send
would be the one most suited to their *spiritual*
requirements. As to granting interviews and so
divulging my identity, I have taken the precaution of
consulting my Master before acceding to such
requests ; and only in a very few instances has he
advised me to do so. It would appear that these
message-and-interview seekers do not realise the
difficulties with which I am faced. Although I fully
gave my readers to understand in the concluding
chapter of *The Initiate* that my Master had gone to
reside in another part of the world and had left me
no address, some of those readers seem to have
assumed that I am in the enviable position of being
able to go and see him whenever I wish, or of ringing
him up on the telephone, or *a* telephone, material or
psychic. But the truth is otherwise, as a perusal of
the first chapter and the epilogue of this book will
show. For one thing my Master now lives thousands
of miles away from my home, and for another I am
at present entirely dependent on *his* wishes for any

communication between us. He knows perfectly all
that is in my consciousness, and hence is fully aware
of my needs and of what letters and requests I receive.
Thus when he feels that a particular individual can
be spiritually helped by an interview with me or a
judiciously worded letter declining such, he establishes
that communication by means of which I am enabled
to ask which course to adopt. In some difficult
cases he has even dictated the letter to me; in others
he has advised me to remind my correspondents of
the occult truth that *when the pupil is ready, the
Master will be forthcoming*, and that although they
may not know it, they are already being watched and
guided.

* * * * * *

A few words of explanation are necessary regarding the text of this sequel to *The Initiate*. The
talks which I have termed lectures were not delivered
in the order in which they appear in the narrative,
my reasons for altering that order being solely ones
of expediency and obedience to the demands of
literary form. Only a few of the many "talks" at
which I was present have been included, and such
parts of these deleted, as were only intended for
initiates of that particular school which my Master
represents. Although I wrote this book several
years ago, my Master told me that the time was
then not ripe for its publication. This delay has
proved fortunate in one sense, for otherwise the
Epilogue could not have been included. should I

state that my Master seldom if ever employed theosophical nomenclature, but confined himself to the Sanscrit terminology. Even for the word Master he usually substituted *Guru*. As, however, many theosophical words are now much in vogue and I wish to avoid the addition of a glossary, I have translated most of *his* more technical terms into the more current theosophical ones.

I may add in conclusion that while writing the present volume, I received a message of approval and encouragement from one of the Himalayan Masters, who expressed himself as much pleased that *The Initiate* should be followed by this sequel. May it prove worthy of so exalted a blessing.

———————

Since the publication of the first edition, my Master has pointed out certain errors due to faulty memory on my part, and also certain passages which have created a false impression. This new edition has therefore been carefully revised.

The
INITIATE
IN THE NEW WORLD

CHAPTER I

SOME twelve years had passed since I last saw my Master (known by the name of Justin Moreward Haig). In his farewell letter to me he had written : " In future another kind of work is allotted to me, and you and I will not be able to meet in the flesh for some time to come, though whenever you need my help I shall be aware of it and shall answer to your call." And certainly he kept his word, though my own faculties are such that I was not always able to reap the full advantage of his promise. There came in fact a time when it seemed as if I were losing those few faculties I had slowly come to possess. The reason for this has since been made known to me, but at the time I was, to say the least, puzzled. To lose the vision of one's Master is indeed a tragedy to those who are in a position to realise what a Master really means to one's entire life. Nevertheless I will do myself the justice of saying that the loss in itself of my meagre faculties failed to trouble me, for he had often impressed on me that the desire for psychic powers proved a stumbling-block on the path to Spiritual Consciousness; unless desired for totally selfless purposes, so I had never made any special effort to develop them. Indeed, although a spiritist friend, suggested that I should "sit for development" in a little circle she had formed, I was unwilling to comply, and argued that if my Master intended me to "see," my powers, such as they were, would be re-awakened in due course.

And then one day I received a type-written envelope with a United States' postage stamp. This caused me no surprise, as I possess one or two acquaintances in America from whom I occasionally get letters. But my astonishment was considerable—I will not mention my other feelings—when on opening that envelope I discovered the following :—

Dated 1920.

My Son,

Now that this incommensurable and blood-thirsty piece of childishness (to which mankind gives the pseudo-dignified name of war !) has reached its end I would suggest that you make the necessary arrange ments to come over here, at least for a period of a few months, and to come as soon as possible. I have a proposal to make to you which concerns your evolution and without which I hardly think it feasible for you to progress much further in this particular incarnation. Although for these few latter years you have not been fully aware of me, I on my part have watched and followed *you* in your inner life, and may tell you without reserve that you have to thank your own *faith* for making possible what I now suggest. True, there may be difficulties in your way, but I ask you only to retain that faith which so far has stood you in good stead, decide to take the voyage, and I promise you assistance will be forthcoming.

My friend, I send you my blessings and await your answer. May you choose wisely, for that is the hope of

Yours always,

J. M. H.

P.S.—Excuse type-written letter—but time is at a premium in this country.

No comment is necessary. There were difficulties to be overcome ; financial ones which at the time seemed insurmountable ; and yet circumstances so arranged themselves that something in the nature of a windfall occurred. To me the Master's word is law, and having in the exuberance of my feelings read and re-read his letter several times, two hours had not passed before I had replied to him. *How* I was to come, exactly when I could come, I was unable to see, but come I would—thus I wrote to him. And within three weeks I was on an Atlantic liner, and what is more, with a larger balance to my credit in the bank than I had had for some years.

I sailed into Boston harbour on a wonderfully crisp sunny autumn morning; and after all the stories that my fellow-passengers had told me, did not look forward to my encounter with the formidable custom-house officials. But almost the moment I disembarked, a buoyant clear-skinned young man accosted me. "Pleased to meet you, Mr. Broadbent."

Puzzled, I shook hands with him, and was about to ask to whom I had the pleasure of speaking, when he enlightened me.

"My name is Arkwright," he said. "I am a *Chela* of Master J. M. H., and have come to offer you any assistance I can. The Master expects you for lunch at one o'clock. In the meantime I'll see you through all this business," pointing to the piles of luggage, "and then take you to your hotel."

"It is extremely good of you to come and meet me," I said warmly, "to tell the truth I was feeling a bit at sixes and sevens. You know how it is when one arrives in a strange place."

" I guess I do," he assented. " Pardon me," and he darted off to some official he had caught sight of, said a few words to him, then returned.

" Now," he assured me, "we shall soon be through ; it's only a matter of waiting till they bring your boxes off the boat."

" Tell me," I asked, while we were waiting, " how did you manage to recognise me ? There is nothing the least distinctive about my appearance."

" Ask me another," was his unelucidating reply, made with a twinkle, " or ask Master. Maybe he'll tell you—or maybe he won't."

I laughed. There was something distinctly humorous about this young American with his matter of fact manner. I wondered how advanced he might be, and what line of occultism appealed to him most, and——

" Your trunk, I believe," he said, indicating a porter crossing the gangway with my property, on which my name was painted.

After that it was all plain sailing. His " friend," the official, made so few difficulties that I suspected some strings had been pulled, but thought it best to ask no questions.

Within less than half an hour, our taxi stopped before a hotel in B—— Street where a room had been engaged for me. Here I unpacked a few of my belongings while my light-hearted companion regaled me with his conversation. Then we set out—to keep my momentous appointment.

My re-meeting with the Master was one of those great moments in life to which my descriptive powers fail to do justice. I had expected much from the long-awaited reunion, but I received even more. The feeling of love and welcome which he managed to convey to me without any great exuberance of words or actions moved me so deeply that, joyful though my emotions were, I was almost relieved when he, realising my embarrassment, dispelled it by adopting a more matter-of-fact tone.

"You stood the test well," he said, "and I am pleased with you."

"Test?" I repeated.

"My son—in an age when psychic powers are rare and hence so greatly desired, it is laudable to view them, or rather their loss, with such philosophic indifference. A child weeps more bitterly over the loss of a new toy than over the loss of an old one."

And then I understood.

In the pause which ensued, I observed my surroundings more closely. J.M.H. was living in a tastefully furnished house in one of those old English-looking squares of Boston. Why a solitary man should require so spacious a residence surprised me at the time; but the reason became apparent in the course of our conversation.

"Not much changed," he resumed, scrutinizing me, "a few more lines, perhaps——"

"Needless to say *you* have not changed at all—except that your hair seems a bit more luxuriant."

He laughed. "All the same, you *will* find me changed when you get to know me in my *American* edition."

"What may that mean?"

"Merely the process of adaptation."

"I am not *very* much the wiser yet," I smiled.

"The methods, the teaching, and even the external manner suited to one country are not suited to another. I must not only adapt my methods to the nationality and the temperament of my pupils, but I must even adapt *myself*. Externally I am not the same man I was in London. Another type of work has been allotted to me, as I wrote to you twelve years ago when I said good-bye."

" It seems curious at first," I commented, " but merely, I suppose, because such an idea never occurred to me before."

" It is absolutely necessary," he emphasised, " and you must not be surprised or disappointed if I say and do things over here which seem at variance with what you knew of me over yonder in Europe.   So I give you this little warning at the outset—it is always well to be prepared."

For the remainder of that interview he talked to me of matters concerning my own evolution, which I do not wish to set down here.   But of one thing I may write, since it will be dealt with later on in its proper place.

There was a particular course of action which my Master desired me to pursue.   " You have not come all this distance," he said, "merely to be near me and receive tuition at my hands. There is something very definite that I wish you to do, as I hinted in my letter.   It will mean a great sacrifice on your part—but it is worth it.   What I have in view for you, I will tell you when the time is ripe ; but that is not yet.   In the meanwhile you will meet most of my pupils. They congregate here every Wednesday evening, when I talk to them. We wish that the spirit of love and brotherhood should exist amongst us all, and by this means we hope to encourage it. After the talk, questions may be asked ; we have conversation, refreshments and smokes. With regard to the latter, we are not fanatical ascetics. With a few exceptions, everyone here has perfect freedom in such matters. We don't believe in interfering with people's comparatively harmless idiosyncrasies—only the taking of alcohol is prohibited. No wine or spirits are served ; against their use I strongly advise my *chelas*. So now you know how things stand. And as to-day is Wednesday, we shall expect you at 8.30."

As it was evident that M.H. was busy, I took my leave, and spent the rest of the day exploring Boston, with a feeling of exhilaration, and a brain busy with many thoughts. What was it that M.H. wished me to do, and which would entail such a sacrifice? A multitude of conjectures presented themselves, but the one which I came later to know was the right one, was not among them.

With regard to that change in himself to

which the Master had alluded, *so far* I had been unable to perceive it.   He was dressed in the same faultless taste as when in London, and the crease down his trousers denoted, if not the same, at any rate an equally painstaking and efficient valet.   But of course it was early in the day to form opinions—I had only seen him for a short time.   What the future had in store, I could not say, but that it held for me a much intensified interest in life, I was certain.

When I returned to the Master's house that evening, I found there some thirty people chatting before settling down for the discourse. M.H. himself moved among them, talking first to one and then to the other; but on seeing me by the door he came forward and introduced me to a young woman and her neighbour.

"This is just to give you a start in," he smiled as he pronounced our names, "but the rule here is that everybody talks to everybody else.   What's the good of all being One unless we behave like it?" he added with humour.

I had, however, little time to profit by my new acquaintanceship, as M.H., going to a chair placed upon a diminutive platform at one end of the room, gave the sign that the talk was about to begin.

CHAPTER II

MORALITY AND SUPERMORALITY

"As most of you know by now, much of the teaching I give you on these evenings is of that nature which may be passed on to those outside our particular Order. To suppose that we Masters exist merely to instruct a few disciples how to develop their psychic centres "—(M.H. used the word *Chakrams*)—"is to suppose a fallacy. Indeed, with the majority of you, I discourage such development as an obstacle to the goal rather than a means of attainment. What we *do* exist for is principally to guide mankind at large and to give forth such moral, spiritual, and ethical ideas as may be required at a particular time. How is this achieved? Through our *chelas*,* who moving in the world and using their discretion, spread such portions of our teaching as they

* Disciples—students—pupils.

deem wise and as opportunity offers.   Thus
we help our disciples, and in return our disciples help us.   If they are writers, some of
that teaching is set forth in their books ; if
they are poets, it appears in their poetry ; if
they are musicians, the spirit of it echoes forth
from their music.   When I look round in this
little community, I see members of various
professions, all of whom help me to the best
of their ability—at least," he added, looking
mischievous, " I *hope* so !   It is to them I also
look for help in bringing new sheep to the fold,
so to say, not only by discreetly spreading our
teachings, but by persuading the incredulous of
the mere fact of our existence.   Of course, no
doubt sensation mongers would much prefer
that we miraculously appeared before our prospective pupils and said : ' I'm your Guru—
come and be my disciple.'   But such is not
our policy and never will be.   Unless the pupil
were clairvoyant and thus could see us without
our having to materialise ourselves, it would
merely involve a waste of force, and incidentally prove us guilty of ' showing off.'   One of
our rules is never to do things in an *extra*-
ordinary way, when they can be done in an
ordinary way.   What we do *after* the disciple

and the Master have become closely linked is another matter."

M. H. lit a cigar.

"To-night I am going to speak of practically *the* greatest obstacle to occult Wisdom"—he used the term Yog Vidya—"spiritual attainment and mystical progress. That obstacle is Conventionality in whatever form it may take, be it in relation to morals or religion. The New Testament writers portrayed the Pharisees as its most typical adherents, and Jesus is reported to have said that the harlots were nearer the kingdom of Heaven than these Pharisees— which, allowing for Oriental hyperbole, is in accordance with fact. If we look at the mental bodies of very conventional people we find their outlines hard and rigid, and the bodies themselves small and as it were under-nourished. When we try to impress those bodies with our teaching our thoughts cannot penetrate the barrier of that hard surface ; and sometimes the only way we can endeavour to break down that barring surface is by music of a modern and rather discordant nature. That is where some modern composers are doing good work.

"From what seeds does this weed of conventionality grow ? From mental laziness, fear

—of what others will think ; vanity—or the capacity to be hurt by what they will say ; and superstition—or the false notion that what the majority think must be right.   Conventionality in its relation to religion need not detain us : what I would discuss this evening is its relation to morals.   As you know, conventional morality exists and is to a greater or lesser degree practised by the masses ; but for the student who is on or about to tread the Path something much more elastic and elevated is required. That something we may christen with the name of *Supermorality*. Whereas the latter is founded on *un*selfishness and obtains its criterion from *un*selfishness, the former all too often, though purporting to be based on unselfishness, is the result of and the excuse for selfishness instead. Thus there are many reasons why people choose to be moral—but there can be only one reason why people choose to be supermoral.   A man may be moral because, as I implied, he fears the aspersions cast upon him by his neighbours— that man is governed by vanity combined with cowardice.   Another man may be moral because it suits his convenience—that is to say because he gets something to his advantage from so-being.   But a man can*not* be supermoral for any such reasons ; on the contrary, what he will reap as far as the world is concerned is likely to be nothing but kicks and calumny. And this because to the individual in the street the super-moralist will often appear as an *im*moralist ; for to the undiscriminating extremes look alike, just as the most dazzling light may be as blinding as the densest darkness."

Here the Master got up from his chair, stepped off the little platform and walked up and down for a while as he talked.

"What, then, is the distinguishing feature between morality and supermorality ? It is self-lessness of motive. The former comes from the brain, the latter from the heart ; the former is dependent on rules and conventions, the latter is entirely dependent on the demands of cir-cumstances. Take such a simple example as deception. Are any of you so innocent as to suppose that even I, whom you are pleased to call your Master, would not and do not deceive you when I think it is for your own good ? Yet there are those who would hold up their hands in horror at such an idea. 'A Master deceive or tell a lie—unthinkable, impossible ! ' They little realise that in one sense a Master needs to act—which is but a form of deceiving

—the greater part of every day. Imagine an Initiate who has acquired that unconditional ever-permanent Love-Consciousness (which, as you know, is a concomitant of Adeptship) behaving in a manner consistent with that inner consciousness? Do you imagine we Initiates dare show the love we feel for everyone? Why, we should probably soon find ourselves in the lunatic asylum, and have to waste our so-called miraculous powers in trying to get out again!"

A ripple of laughter went through the little assembly.

It is all very well for those much-talked-of Mahatmas who live the lives of hermits in the fastnesses of the Himalayas : *they* can behave as they like . . . at least they *could*, if they really did live as hermits—but as a matter of fact many of them don't. They too have got their *Chelas* around them and do not spend the whole day in ecstatic contemplation. That might be very pleasant for *them*—having reached the end of their journey—but how about the poor creatures who are still struggling along the road? Just because we have learnt to do a certain thing— yes, and perhaps taken years, even centuries in the learning of it, does that mean that we must be continually doing that thing, firstly because

of the pleasure it gives us, and secondly in order
to show others that we *can* do it ?   No.   The
supermoralist realises that when he has acquired
a virtue or a faculty, be it truthfulness or ecstatic
trance—what matter—then is the time to hide
it or indulge in it sparingly, or both, as circumstances dictate.   A Swami I once met told me
that in a previous incarnation I had been a
great orator.   Maybe that is true, maybe not ;
but suppose it were true, and I still possessed
great oratorical faculties, would it be fitting for
me to arouse your emotions with great orations
instead of merely talking to you as I do ?   If the
latter method suffices why employ the former ?
By so doing shouldn't I only be reminding you
that I could do something which you can't do ?
Most people, when they acquire a particular
virtue, are inclined to flaunt it in the faces of
those who have not yet acquired it.   They
argue that it is so good for these poor virtueless
persons—little dreaming that vanity is the cause
of their thought.   How would you like it if you
were starving and one of your friends came up
to you with a large slice of cake in his hand,
and proceeded to eat it before your eyes ? . . .
Would that be a kind action ?   Or let us say a
friend of yours had recently lost every cent he

possessed, would you just stand in front of
him and jingle the coins in your pocket for
his benefit? Yet thousands of highly moral
and religious people do this very thing with
their virtues. Ah yes, there a fine lot of
virtue-exhibitions in the world, and you needn't
pay any entrance-fee to look at them. But
what do all these virtue-exhibitions really
imply? Simply that one man or woman wants
to lord it over another. 'A virtue is a virtue,'
they argue, 'therefore the oftener it comes into
the limelight the better '—and then they'll probably quote scripture to themselves to substan-
tiate their argument." The Master paused and
then continued with an altered inflection :

" But are there *never* times when we should
show our virtues? Well, of course there are,
but all depends on why, how, and where we
show them. There are also times when we
should show our vices—even vices we don't
possess. Recently a *chela* came to me and
asked how he could cure a friend who had started
the drink habit. And I gave him some advice
which entailed breaking our rules. How did he
proceed in accordance with that advice? He
went and got drunk several times in company
with his friend. One night before either he or

his friend were too drunk to be completely fuddled, he threw his glass on the floor and said: 'Look here, why on earth do we drink this damned filthy stuff? It tastes rotten, gives us a putrid headache, and isn't worth it. I'm going to chuck it, why don't you chuck it too?' And that man *did* 'chuck it.' His friend's action had such a strong suggestive value, combined with a little occult assistance I rendered, that he was cured. From a conventional-moral standpoint my disciple broke our rules, deceived his friend, and made a beast of himself, as the phrase goes; but from a supermoral standpoint, he acted like a heroic Samaritan. Thus what you need to make people realise is that there is no absolutely permanent moral truth—and please do not confound moral truths with spiritual truths; the latter *are* permament, but the former are dependent on a variety of changing things. For instance the morals of Thibet are not the morals of New York. If here in the States a woman married not merely Mr. X. but all his brothers as well, she would be looked upon as a sink of depravity. If, on the contrary, in Thibet she refused to marry all those brothers, she would be looked upon as something equally reprehensible. And it is no use merely arguing that the Thibetans are barbarians and the New Yorkers are not—that isn't the reason. The reason is simply that in Thibet there are not enough women to go round. What's more, if this fantastic war had lasted much longer, there might not have been enough *men* to go round in this country, and so then a man would not only have had to marry his sweetheart, but all her sisters as well. You laugh, and rightly so, for everything has its humorous side ; but your less enlightened compatriots wouldn't laugh at such an unprecedented state of affairs. They'd say it was intensely and disgustingly immoral. Yet let us be honest and courageous enough to look facts in the face. Is it more evil to go out and kill hundreds of innocent individuals because nations have got themselves into a mess through refusing to love their neighbours, or is it more evil to marry several women to save the population from the result of that mess ? Let moralists answer me *that*. Personally I hold no two opinions on the subject. But I'll tell you why moralists would *think* they disagree with me. ' It's because for centuries that type of killing on a gigantic scale has been regarded as something grandiose and heroic. Why a thing which is evil on a small scale should be justifiable

when augmented to a colossal scale is a question
you mustn't ask a logician ; but I'll tell you the
cause of that inconsistency—it lies in the one
word convention, or tradition if you prefer it."

"And so you must realise that we who are trying to tread the path of Wisdom cannot take the
same view of morals as the world at large takes;
that we require something more elevated, more
elastic, more spiritual ; that in view of the
fact that morals not only change with place and
nation and climate, but also with the times themselves, we require a criterion different from
mere moral tradition, of what is right and wrong.
And if some people are not disposed to believe
that morals change with the times, then let them
look into the book held most sacred by all the
peoples of the West, and read how at one time
the idea of Justice was ' An eye for an eye, and
a tooth for a tooth.'   Or look further back still
and read of King Solomon, said to be the wisest
—which surely also implies the most moral—
man who ever lived.   But tell me this : how
would the bulk of fastidious Americans with
their legislation against this, that and the other,
regard a man who had seven hundred wives and
two hundred concubines ?   Would they consider
him the wisest man on this whole continent ?

I should like to know how even he could find the time to cultivate wisdom, under the stress of such extensive erotic obligations." Loud laughter greeted this but the Master continued unmoved : "And by the way, since we have touched on the subject of legislation, I may point out that no supermoralist ever interferes with the liberty of other people—only moralists do that. By all means let men make as many laws as they like if it amuses them, but let them make them for *themselves*, and not for others. What business have we to go poking our fingers into other people's pies ? Do you think that by *forcing* our fellows to do this or that, we are furthering their evolution ? Are you furthering the evolution of a prize-fighter by tying up his hands? No. There is only one way to further the evolution of your fellows, and that is by *persuading* them— not by forcing them, mind you—to alter their motives : for motive is everything, actions are secondary. If you can teach people to think with their hearts as well as with their brains, you'll have done some good."

This ended the discourse for the evening, but the Master resumed his seat.

"Anybody want to ask any questions ?" he said.

" How would you define a spiritual truth ? " the girl next to me enquired. " You said we mustn't mix up spiritual truths with moral truths."

" When the Yogi maintains All is Brahman," came the answer, "he is uttering a spiritual truth. Or when we say there is only one Self—that is a spiritual truth. Such truths are permanent, unchanging ; moral truths are relative, and hence subject to change. Any more questions ? "

No one responded, so the Master stepped down from the little platform, and the company got up from their chairs. There was a buzz of conversation, and a movement towards the long table at the side of the room on which were spread light refreshments. I was offered sandwiches by an exceedingly pretty girl who, in the most natural manner in the world "made friends" with me, telling me first of all " how very glad they were to have me amongst them, and that she hoped I had come to stay, etc., etc." A few others followed suit and said very much the same thing, their object obviously being to make me feel "at home," in which they certainly succeeded.

Most of the pupils I took to be under forty-

five, but a few of them were over that age,
and one I took to be verging on sixty.   I was
especially struck by their healthy clean-blooded
appearance, although none could be described
as " beefy " or particularly muscular.

The spirit of *bonhomie* was particularly evident amongst them, and I may here remark
that during the several months I spent with
them, not once did I encounter anything approaching malicious gossip.

After about half an hour's conversation, the
little gathering showed signs of thinning out.
One or two of the guests shook hands with
M H. before going home, but the majority,
I noticed, just took " French leave " or shouted
a "Good-night to you all."   As I was in hopes
of making an appointment with M.H. for
the following day, I lingered behind and exchanged a few words with him.

"Well, this is how we do things *here*," he
said genially, "hope you made some friends?"

I told him everybody had been very nice
to me.

" There are one or two I'd like you to meet
in a more intimate way.   Let me see, now,"
he reflected, "to-morrow's Thursday—Viola
Brind is coming at five, and bringing along a

friend who may become a pupil. Yes, that will do. Turn up at five o'clock too, you'll find tea going. Afterwards when the others have gone we can have a chat."

We said good-night to each other.

As I passed through the hall, I encountered a Hindoo next to whom I had sat; he was collecting his belongings.

"Going my way?" I asked.

"Which is your way?"

"Towards B—— Street."

He told me he *was* going that way, and I suggested we should walk along together. He was a powerfully built man with the most beautifully cut features I had ever seen, and I wondered as we walked if he were very advanced. Talkative he certainly was not, yet his silence gave no impression of unfriendliness.

"You have been long with the Master?" I asked.

"Yes," he replied, suppressing the beginnings of the kind of smile that is apt to appear when children ask a naïve question.

"Then I suppose you've gone very far?"

This time he did not suppress his smile. "All things are relative," he answered non-commitally.

I am not inquisitive by nature, but if information concerning my Master is anywhere within reach, I grab at it like a hungry boy at an apple; so I persisted. " Do they all practice Yoga here? "

" What do you understand by Yoga? "

" Why, posture, breathing-exercises, meditation."

" No, not all," he looked at me benignly and asked : " Can the elephant suck honey like the bee, or the mongoose carry a rider like the horse? "

I supposed not, and was inwardly amused at his similes.   " Then what methods does M.H. employ? "

" Those which are best suited to each disciple ; and they are as many and varied as the temperaments and occupations of the disciples themselves."

And that was all I got from him, as we had already reached his apartments, or whatever they were.   To my regret I never saw him again.   I learned afterwards that he had sailed for India the very next day.

But that first night I was to run across yet another of the pupils.   I found him sitting in the lounge of my hotel, reading the paper.

He was a musician who was touring in the
United States, and put in an appearance at
M.H.'s whenever he got the chance.

"Seen each other already once to-night," he
said, nodding cheerfully, "have a seat—and a
talk before turning in?"

"By all means," I answered, realising at a
glance that he would be more communicative
than my Hindoo friend.

"Where did *you* meet M.H.?" I enquired
without any preamble.

"In London, through a friend of mine.
And you?"

"Also in London."

"Then you've known him quite a time?"

I nodded assent.   "Who was that very
impressive-looking Hindoo?   I walked a bit
of the way with him."

"Oh, that's Yogi ——" he mentioned a long
Sanscrit name; "he's a wonderful fellow."

"He certainly carries a wonderful atmosphere about with him," I agreed, "struck me
as very advanced."

"Yes, he *is*, but you'll find out in time that
some of the people who may not *strike* you as
very advanced, are the most advanced of all.
That Yogi, by the way, was a hermit in the

Jungle for ten years and never spoke a word for three, so I'm told."

"Yet M.H. is his Guru instead of one of the Indian Masters—that seems curious."

"You'll come up against a lot of curious things here. I've long given up trying to solve riddles. Still, this one is easy enough, I think. Do you suppose this is the first life in which you have met M.H.?"

"No."

"Well, then, since the link between Guru and *Chela* is the strongest in the world, it persists life after life, doesn't it?"

I agreed.

"Now, do you really think that because in this incarnation M.H. was born in England and his *Chela* in India, it can make any difference?"

"No, of course not, now you put it that way."

"Besides," he went on, "M.H. was in India for years and years."

"Good God, then how old can he be?" I exclaimed.

"Oh, about a hundred," he replied with impish carelessness; then, correcting himself: "No, as a matter of fact only about two of the *Chelas* know, and they won't let on." He hummed a

tune and drummed with his fingers on the arm
of his chair.   I offered him a cigarette.

"No use to me, thanks," he said.   "I don't
smoke."

"What—not allowed to?"

"There's no *allowed* here—in *that* connection
—I'm *advised* not to : it aggravates an obscure
and obstinate complaint I've got."

"Can't M.H. cure it for you?"

"You mean *won't* . . .   When I've learnt to
ignore it and work as efficiently as if I hadn't
got it, he'll put me on to the cure.   He says—
well, you know how he says these things—
'My son, it is a greater achievement to do good
work in spite of a sick body, than to cure the
body itself.'"

"I thought that Buddha said that perfect
health was necessary to attain salvation."

"Perhaps he did, and I daresay in our final
incarnation we shall have splendid health.   I
don't know about *you*," he added humorously,
"but *I've* got a long way to go before then."

"Good Lord, *me* . . ." I exclaimed, "all the
same, you know, Ramakrishna was a pretty big
saint, and he died of cancer."

"Yes, because he used to take on other people's
Karma.   But even he wasn't a Master."

"How do you know that?"

"M.H. told me. He said he was nearing Adeptship but hadn't reached it yet."

"Does Master expect his *Chelas* to study philosophical books for a certain time every day, as they do in some esoteric schools?" I asked after a pause.

The musician burst out laughing. "We are not learning the occult alphabet : most of us have done all that before we came here. I used to read for about three or four hours a day before I met M.H.—not as a duty, but because I liked it. When you've extracted all the knowledge you can out of books, then the Master appears. He says the people who write the books only *know* up to a point. Why, the sort of rules that are laid down in the books are quite unsuited to certain people, and even do harm. I've read, somewhere, for instance, that unless you meditate for half an hour a day, you can't lead the spiritual life. *I'm* told not to meditate more than five minutes, because that sort of concentration needs too much force, and M.H. says all the force I have must go into my work."

"I'm learning a lot to-night," I remarked, meaning it sincerely, "it's a piece of good luck I ran across you."

He laughed again. "There's no such thing as luck. *He* told me to hang about here to-night—considering we *are* staying at the same hotel. We're encouraged to talk and discuss things among ourselves, and especially when anyone new turns up. Of course," he added parenthetically, "we all may have our individual secrets, but if we don't know how to hold our tongues about those, so much the worse for us. He told us one day that sometimes we might learn far more by talking among ourselves than by listening to *him*. I take that with a large pinch of salt—you know how modest he is—but I've found some truth in it all the same."

"Well, I hope we shall often meet for more talks."

"I hope so too—I only wish to God I wasn't off again the day after to-morrow for two or three months—I'd stick around here for ever if I got the chance. Still, as he says these journeys are on *his* work, I have to console myself with *that*. After all——" he broke off with a gesture.

We sat talking for another two hours, and would not have gone to bed even then, if the hotel-servants hadn't come and glared at us for wasting the light.

CHAPTER III

MISS BRIND AND MISS DELAFIELD

When I arrived at the Master's house the following afternoon I was shown into a little study on the ground floor, where I found him seated at his desk before a number of type-written letters which he was evidently in the act of signing. It was a cosy room lined with hundreds of books, mostly on occult subjects, as I afterwards discovered.

"Punctual to the minute," he said genially as he got up from his chair and greeted me. "Well, how have you been amusing yourself? Seen much of Boston yet?"

I told him I'd spent most of the day writing letters to England announcing my safe arrival.

"How else should you arrive?" he said with one of his twinkles, "you don't suppose we'd ask you to come over here and then let you get shipwrecked on the way, do you?"

"*I* don't," I laughed, "but my mother and friends can't be expected to know that, now can they?"

"Well, perhaps not," he conceded.

The servant announced : " Miss Brind, Miss Delafield."

M.H. shook hands with them both, introduced us and offered them chairs.   I recognised Miss Brind as one of the pupils I had seen the previous evening but Miss Delafield was new to me.   The former was a small but well-proportioned blonde, with what would be described as a clever face rather than a good-looking one.   The latter—well, at my age I am not easily set a-flame, but I do not exaggerate when I say that she was so startlingly beautiful that I was completely bowled over.

"So this is your friend," M.H. said cheerily to Miss Brind, but looking at Miss Delafield. " I understand you are interested in our work."

" I am *more* than interested," she smiled.

" May I ask your age ? "

" Thirty," was the unhesitating answer.

" Have you been or are you a member of any occult society—theosophical, for instance ? "

" No, never."

"You have read a lot of books on the subject?"

" Yes, a good many."

" What, for example ? "

" Swami Vivekananda's.   My mother used to know him."

" Ah, I see.   And has anybody helped you at all ? "

" My mother and Viola—Miss Brind."

M.H. gazed at her intently for a moment. "What is your object in studying these things?" he asked in a casual tone.

Miss Delafield look puzzled. "My object . . .? Well, really, I don't quite know ; there seem to be such a lot.   It makes you look at life differently, and it's so thrilling.   Besides, it's so useful to help other people with."

M.H. seemed pleased, and glanced at her approvingly.   " When did you begin studying this kind of philosophy ? " he asked.

" Three years ago."

" H'm, that's not very long, is it ? " he said kindly.

" No, perhaps it isn't."

" You see it doesn't give you much chance to know whether it's merely a phase or not.   You might tire of it."

Miss Delafield looked a trifle disconcerted, and my sympathy went out to her.   " I don't think it's very likely," she said, "but of course you can judge of that better than I can."

"What makes you think that?"

"I am not totally ignorant about Masters," she gave him a knowing little smile.

He laughed. "I shouldn't take too much for granted if I were you."

"But I don't think I am."

"Well, the long and the short of it is you want a teacher," he said in a business-like tone.

"Yes, but the point is not do I want the teacher but does he want *me*. I mean," she hastily corrected, "does he think I'm—I'm likely to be a worthy pupil?"

The Master leant forward and patted her hand. "That's all right. Miss Brind hasn't left us quite in the dark about you"—Miss Delafield shot a grateful glance at her friend— "The thing is, will you be able to put up with our ways? We call a spade a spade here; if you're at all squeamish . . ."

"Oh, I'm used to that," she said laughing, "I've got three brothers."

"Very well then, we'll expect you at our Wednesday evening classes. And now for tea," he added, pressing the bell.

Miss Delafield tried to express her gratitude,

but the Master waved it aside. " I have a certain amount of time at my disposal," he explained, "and I'm glad to give some of it to those who need it."

The servant brought in tea and placed it in front of Miss Brind who proceeded to do the honours.

" By the way," said M.H., "our friend here has come over from England to be with us for a time ; if either of you can introduce him to some of your acquaintances I shall be grateful."

They said they would be only too glad.

"There are some of the University people he might care to know," he suggested, " Mr. Broadbent is a poet."

Immediately they appeared interested ; Americans are incorrigible hero-worshippers.

" I write poetry," I said laughing, "but I don't know that that constitutes being a poet."

The Master went to one of the shelves and brought out two volumes of my poetry, which he handed to the ladies.

" Really . . . ," I protested "and such old stuff too ! "

" But I've *read* these," declared Miss Delafield with surprised enthusiasm, " I've admired your poems for a long time. Fancy meeting you like this—I *am* glad to know you!"

"I'd no idea my work had penetrated so far," I said, pleased to have found a bond of sympathy with this beautiful girl.

"If ever Master admires a thing," Miss Brind threw in, "it always *goes*."

M.H. looked on amused. "That's one of your superstitions, my child."

"Oh, no, it isn't," she retorted with a laugh. "There are very few of us," turning to me, "who don't know your poems. Master often quotes them and says there's a lot of occult wisdom in them."

"He pays them a compliment," I said, and meant it in a very real sense. What greater compliment could I wish for my work than the approval of a Master?

"I've still to hear him pay a compliment," she maintained, looking at him quizzically. "Now *do* you pay compliments?"

He made a non-committal gesture. "Well, perhaps not very often. Depends what you mean by the word compliment." He took the two books and put them back in the shelves. Then he pulled out a third one, and held it up for me to look at. "You see we are quite up to date! This man, like many writers," he came and stood with his back to the fireplace, "possesses the laudable quality of being unusually modest. He wrote a history of a friend of his in which he figured to a considerable extent, but never once mentioned that he himself wrote poetry."

Miss Delafield gave me an admiring look.

"Why on earth should I?" I exclaimed, "I was writing about my friend, not myself." M.H. and I exchanged glances.

"Mayn't we know the name of the book?" asked Miss Brind.

"For heaven's sake let's change the conversation," I said, laughing to hide my confusion, for I was uncertain whether M.H. would like even his pupils to know of *The Initiate*. "All this talk about my own wretched productions is most embarrassing."

Fortunately a knock at the door rescued me.

"Come in," said the Master.

It was Arkwright with a note which he handed to M.H. He shook hands with us while the latter, after excusing himself, read it. It was, I gathered, very brief, for in less than a minute he said: "Say yes, eleven o'clock," waved his hand, and Arkwright went out immediately.

Miss Brind glanced at her watch and then significantly at her friend. They both got up to go.

"Will you lunch with me at my club on Saturday?" Miss Brind asked while Miss Delafield was saying good-bye to M. H.

I told her I would be delighted, and she gave me the address.

"And with me to-morrow at my home," from Miss Delafield, "my mother and I would be so happy."

Again I said I would be delighted.

"That'll be lovely. I am sure you will enjoy my mother," she added—the first American idiom I had noticed.

"I'm sure I shall," I agreed, bowing.

M. H. opened the door for them.

"You must excuse my holding you up as a paragon of modesty," he laughingly confided to me when they had gone, "but I'm up against a national weakness here—it's in the blood; ingrained *lack* of modesty. Even the best of them are not quite free from it."

"Oh, if *that* was the reason ——"

"There is a subtle connection between hero-

worship and conceit, though one wouldn't suppose it.   If you think another man very
wonderful for what he can do, you're apt to
think the same of yourself if you can do
likewise.   Have a cigar?"

"That's a very ingenious psychological reflection," I said, accepting the cigar, "it certainly never struck me before.   But, I say
really—you nearly landed me in difficulties
about that book!"

"How so?" he took a cigar himself.

"You don't want people to know it's about
you, do you?"

"People and pupils are somewhat different.
Most of my pupils have learnt discretion."

"But what about new ones?"

"Miss Delafield?"

I nodded.

"I can *see*."

I laughed at my own foolishness.   "By
George, she *is* beautiful!" I exclaimed.

M.H. raised his eyebrows knowingly.   "Lost
your heart, eh?"

"Very *nearly*."

"One day, if you carry out the program
I have in view for you, I hope and think you
will lose it permanently."

"What may that mean ?"

"Permanent Love-consciousness."

"What—love everybody ?"

"Certainly."

"Do you mean to say there's a chance for *me* to get that ?"

"If—you carry out my program."

I was conscious of a thrill. "But you haven't said what that program is!"

He shook his head. "Patience, my son." He put his hand for a moment on mine.

"I thought only Masters could have permanent Love-Consciousness ?"

"Not correct. You can have Love-Consciousness for several lives before you reach Masterhood. This life, say you reach it at fifty; the next earlier; the next earlier still, till you're finally born with it. In *that* life you'll reach Masterhood. But of course there is no absolute rule as to time. Why set limitations? Do your utmost, and you progress all the quicker." He paused for a moment. "But it's not only Love-Consciousness I've got in view for you—there are your poems."

"My poems . . . ?"

"You are a far greater poet than you imagine."

"It's nice to hear it from *you*," I said, "but, as

a matter of fact, I've been infernally dissatisfied with my work of late."

"That is merely because you are subconsciously aware that something much bigger is coming through later on—*if*, as I say, you carry out my program."

"But *of course* I shall carry out your program."

"I hope and think so," he said again.

There was another knock at the door.   M.H. went out and spoke to somebody in the hall. "In a few minutes," he said round the door, as he closed it and came back into the room.

"You have another appointment?" I asked. He nodded.

I got up from my chair.   "When can I see you again?"

"To-morrow there is a talk on Mantrams at 8.30.   Always keep Wednesday and Friday evenings free—those are the two days for the classes.   But wait a minute—there's to-morrow morning.   I've got to drive out to a little place in the vicinity here.   If you care to come for the run——?"

"I'd love it."

"Well, call for me at, say 11.30.   There are two Orientals coming at 11 to pay their respects to me."   He smiled ironically.   "I shall have had quite enough of their respects in half an hour, so just walk in and that will be the most charitable hint we can give them to get up and go."

I laughed, but asked, slightly apprehensive: "I suppose we can be back by 1.15 all right? I'm lunching with Miss Delafield."

"Ah, that's very important," he teased me, "don't worry, I'll drop you at the door. By the way—got anything to read? If not," with a wave of his arm towards the shelves, "help yourself. Au revoir." He went out briskly.

CHAPTER IV

THE ORIENTALS AND THE MOTOR-DRIVE

I imagined the two Orientals whom I found next morning conversing with M. H. to be Mongolians. After greetings had been exchanged— they did not shake hands with me—they resumed their conversation with the Master in what I assumed was not Hindoostani. Certainly I did not understand a word of it. But the circumstance led me to wonder how many languages my Master could speak. I knew he was conversant with Italian, French, German, and Sanscrit, not to mention English, but that he added current Oriental languages to his list was new to me. Whatever this particular language was, it was evident that he spoke it very fluently, for he was the principal talker in that somewhat unusual interview.

It must have been about five minutes after

my arrival that the two Oriental gentlemen showed signs of moving.   Then an unexpected thing happened : they prostrated themselves at my Master's feet.   And at that moment I got a glimpse of him—from yet another angle.   As he looked down at their prostrate figures, he glanced at me out of the corner of his eye for a second, and winked!   The action was so irresistibly humorous that I had the greatest difficulty not to burst out laughing.   As it was, I had to resort to blowing my nose in order to hide the twitching of my mouth.

"You nearly did for me," I said when the visitors had left.

He raised his eyebrows.

"That wink. . . ."

"Oh, that!" he laughed.   "Have a smoke?"

I accepted a cigar.

"The motor is at the door, so we'll be off now, I think.   Got a warm coat with you?"

I told him I had.

The drive was exhilarating.   M.H. took the wheel himself, and we dashed through the crisp autumn air at a speed which in England would have endangered our licence.   But the Master proved himself a splendid chauffeur, and after we had got away from the noise of the busier

streets, kept up a lively conversation at the
same time.

"How did you like Miss Brind?" he asked.

"She seems a very pleasant sort of creature,"
I answered without great enthusiasm.

"She's a highly evolved soul," he assured me,
"I should like you to cultivate her."

"Certainly, if *you* wish it."

"You can help each other."

"It'll be more a question of her helping *me*,
I think.   She's probably much more advanced
than I am."

"That is a matter *I* can judge better than
you."

I was silent—but grateful for what I took to
be an expression of approval.

"To tell you the truth," I admitted after a
pause, "I found her friend so astonishingly
beautiful that she rather put Miss Brind in the
shade."

He smiled enigmatically.

"You don't think she's beautiful?"

"You see, I'm a little less dependent on faces
and figures for the spectacle of beauty than—
well, the majority of people.   If one can see all
the subtler bodies as well as the physical, the
latter loses some of its significance."

We whizzed round a corner and had to pull up sharp to avoid a cart, and I couldn't help wondering why Masters didn't make use of their psychic vision on all occasions. If a Master can see into the future, I argued, surely he can see round a corner. I put to him what was in my mind.

"You forget," was his answer, "that only those who have no more Karma to work off can take the initiation for Masterhood. Accidents, so-called, in which a person gets killed or hurt are purely matters of Karma, so why should I use psychic vision when it isn't necessary? If we can get across a river by the bridge, why walk on the water like St. Peter?"

"Are you *ever* stumped?" I asked, realising that he had an answer for everything.

"*Ever* is a big word. There *is* an answer to most questions, but it's not always wise to give it. Sometimes we can teach people far more by keeping back the truth than by telling it. If you tell a conceited man that he's potentially divine, it's true, but it's likely to make him more conceited still; so you'll certainly not be teaching him modesty in that way. Even with my *chelas*, I have to be very careful until they are far advanced. That's why you'll hear me say very little over here about astral bodies and the astral plane. Level-headedness and good sound common-sense are what I try to instil into my pupils before I encourage them to peep into the hidden realms. A thorough grounding in philosophy is the first thing to be acquired—otherwise one's up against hysteria and imagination of a wrong type, and all the other evils we know so well. I know of women who come down to breakfast every morning with the story of some wonderful vision they've had in the night, in which some supposed 'Master' has appeared and given them 'teaching.' And when you come to ask what the 'teaching' was, it turns out to be sheer nonsense or some moral platitude. Well, well—it is fortunate we *gurus* have a sense of humour."

We pulled up at a large house standing in a garden overlooking the river.

" Here we are," he said, getting out of the car. " I shan't be more than a quarter of an hour. Please wait out here."

As he disappeared into the house I wondered who lived there. Was it a pupil, and if so why did M. H. have to go to *him* instead of his coming to M. H.? Still I determined to ask no questions. After all what business was it of

mine ?   If he wanted to tell me, he would do so,
if not—

Then suddenly my thoughts turned to what
lay before me—my luncheon engagement. Miss
Delafield—what a euphonious name ! Had she
an equally euphonious christian name ? Would
she attract me as much at our second meeting
as at our first ?   But was it our *first* ?   I felt as
if I had known her in a previous life. The
secret of my sudden feeling for her could not
arise solely from her beauty. I had known so
many beautiful women, yet not one of them had
really touched my heart. Supposing I fell passionately in love, what would M.H. say ? I did
not for a moment doubt his tolerance and understanding, but would it be quite "playing the
game" to start a love-affair with one of his *chelas*,
especially at *my* age ? He might make allow-
ances for young people, but for a man approaching fifty . . . . ! As to marriage—for one thing,
I hated the idea ; for another I looked upon it
as an obstacle, having read in one of the theosophical books that occultists ought not to marry.
Besides which I was too old not to have learnt
that love seldom lasts. Illusions on that score
I had none. There were also what I took to be
my Master's views on the subject. I could not

imagine that he wanted me to marry—he had never hinted at such a possibility. If it had been his intention that I should do so, surely he would have told me in England while I was still young enough. There was for instance Gertrude Wilton. In the episode connected with her he had assisted me by pacifying an irate and selfish father, and in this manner had smoothed the way for me, but as to my marrying Gertrude—he had taken for granted that I did *not* wish to marry her.

All these thoughts had passed through my mind as I stood leaning on a railing idly watching the river, and listening to the gentle flow of the water against the banks. I had in fact been so engrossed that I had not heard M. H. come out of the house, and his voice telling me he was ready startled me.

" That comes of playing with fire without having a fireman handy," he observed, getting into the car.

I glanced at him enquiringly.

" A man got himself into such a deep trance," he explained as we started off, " that I had to go and get him out of it. A *chela* of mine asked me to go ; the doctors were stumped. They'd have put the man under the earth in a day or two. However, please keep your mouth shut ; those people in here think I'm merely a heart-specialist. I suppose they'll be writing to know what my fee is next," he laughed.

" But do they know your address ? "

" They'll try and get at me through my *chela.*"

" And what'll you do about it ? "

" Accept it and give it to a charity, I guess."

"Why, you've caught a bit of American," I exclaimed.

"Caught it—no. *Adopted* it. The saying is trite, but in Rome do as Rome does. You can get much nearer to people's hearts if you adopt their own ways. I've heard it said over here that our English seems rather affected to the American ear. A little *superior*, in fact. Well, that'll never do. Anything that savours of putting on airs is to be tabood in my sort of situation."

" You really are a splendid actor," I said, and evoked a laugh at my enthusiasm; "if you didn't look quite unaltered and hadn't the same voice I could hardly believe you were the same person. Apart from any Americanisms you don't seem to talk the same language."

" One must go with the times. If I talked as people did when I was a boy the effect would

be stilted.   I'm not quite so young as I look,
you know."

Again I wondered what his age might be,
but refrained from asking.

"What, after all, do externals matter?" he continued, "externals are changing every moment
of our lives, yet some people are so *afraid* of
changing."

" It's a curious thing," I observed irrelevantly,
"but somebody once told me that all Adepts
were pretty much alike."

"In consciousness —yes; but not in externals.
Each Adept will have his own little character-
istics and mannerisms, as well as the character-
istics of his race and nationality.   Look at some
of these Indian Swamis who have still a fair way
to go before they reach Adeptship—externally
they are as calm as tortoises; they'll sit for
hours in a chair without moving.   But that
astonishing calm lies in the race, not in the
individual.   It is a species of oriental indolence
and not necessarily mind-concentration.   Why,
I know an Adept who sometimes fidgets with
his watch-chain and dangles his legs over the
side of a chair and behaves almost like a school-
boy. And why not? Only vain people are always
thinking of their dignity—unless it happens to

be a racial characteristic, as with the Arabs. A
woman once said to me, talking of that very
man : ' I'm sure he can't be an Adept—no
Adept would ever do anything in bad taste.'

" ' No,' I remarked casually, ' except when in
the company of those who are *obsessed* with the
idea of good taste, and cannot be cured except
by the hardening system ! ' "

I laughed, and then we both relapsed into
silence as we got back into the town, the noise
of the traffic making conversation difficult. But
as we arrived at Miss Delafield's door he said,
with one of his whimsical smiles : " These little
' flutters ' are sometimes useful to poets—they
assist inspiration."

I could have embraced him.   With that one
sentence he had set my mind at ease.

CHAPTER V

MISS DELAFIELD AND MISS BRIND

If I were writing this book about myself I should have no compunction in relating the details of that little luncheon-party, but since my sole object is to portray the personality and philosophy of my Master in what he himself humorously described as his American edition, I must omit the non-essentials. As he has permitted me to include some of his discourses in this volume it is necessary that I should economise in space, and metaphorically use the blue pencil on all portions which have little relation to himself.

Therefore suffice it to say that the impression created upon me the previous day by Clare Delafield was only enhanced when I came to know her better. In addition to her quite extraordinary beauty, she had a quick intelligence and a broadness of outlook which made

me realise at once that despite the difference in
our ages I *could* entertain feelings for her other
than those inspired by romantic admiration.
She possessed—at least I imagined so—the
pre-requisites to real companionship. We
talked mostly of Yoga philosophy, and it was
evident to me that as well as having studied
deeply, she had brought a good deal of in-
dependent thought to bear on the subject, as
also on the one or two other subjects we discussed. Her love of poetry, for instance, was
absolutely genuine, and she won my heart by
immediately hitting on what *I* myself considered to be the best lines in my own work.
Altogether, there appeared to be a distinct
bond of sympathy between us, and one which
my intuition, together with a few external signs
—trifling to onlookers but significant to me—
told me she was as fully aware of as I was
myself. The fact that I should have entered
Miss Delafield's house for the first time at one-
fifteen and not left it till six-thirty, can hardly
be considered without its significance either,
especially as I am not one of those inconvenient
people who never seem to realise when it is
time to take their departure. I had made
several attempts—albeit quite against my in-

clination—to end my visit, but had been met with : "Why must you go ? It would be just lovely of you to stay on." So each time I only too gladly gave in and did stay on. Moreover Mrs. Delafield herself gave me a plausible excuse to do so. Almost immediately after lunch she had expressed her regret, but she "was obliged to attend a tiresome commitee-meeting," and hoped I would not dream of leaving until she came back. And fortunately for me she did not come back till nearly five o'clock, during which time I enjoyed an uninterrupted *tête-à-tête* with her daughter. When at last I did get up to go, I was told to regard Nr. —— Hudson Street as "open house," and to visit its two inmates—there was no Mr. Delafield— as often as I felt inclined; the oftener the better. In addition " If I cared to have Clare show me some of the country in the motor," as her mother expressed herself, "she wo ld be so happy." In fact "anything they could do for me, a lonely bachelor in a strange town, I need only tell them," and so on and so forth.

Thus, when I eventually walked back to my hotel, it was with the agreeable feeling expressed in the phrase "to have fallen on one's feet." I had not only met with the warmest

hospitality and with every prospect of its con-
tinuance, but had received that hospitality from
at any rate *one* who had already awakened
sentiments within me of a most romantic nature.
In a word, Clare Delafield, even though I had
only known her—in this life—one day, had
already coloured my consciousness, and I was
aware of an inner exhilaration which, as the
Master had implied, might impel me once again
to express myself in verse.   To me creative
sterility spelt a state of mind which only writers
can realise.   To be barren of ideas is to be only
half alive, and for this reason I heartily endorse
the statement—though who made it I have forgotten—that there are only two vital things in
life ; one is work and the other is love.   If we
can have the two together, then the height of
joy is ours.

   That evening I attended the talk on Mantrams
and the following day had lunch with Miss Brind
at her club, as had been previously arranged.

   Although she did not attract me, and would
not even have attracted me if my sentiments
had not been centred elsewhere, I realised immediately that we could become very good
friends.   She was witty and vivacious as well
as highly intelligent and well-read.   In addition

I discovered that she possessed natural psychic faculties of a no mean order, and that she wrote mystical books. Although I had not taken much notice of her at our first meeting, I remember having got the impression that she was not an American, and this proved to be correct. She was English, had been born in London, had lived there the greater part of her life, and would return there in the course of a few months. She had come over to the States at the suggestion of her Master. In fact, over our luncheon she told me a most romantic story.

Already in her childhood—she was now thirty-three—she had seen clairvoyantly the figure of M.H. who used to appear at her bedside. Her parents to whom she spoke of this, had laughed at her and considered her fanciful, but the attempts to convince her that the vision she saw was purely imaginary, had no effect whatever. "She had seen what she had seen," and *their* ignorance could not convince *her* knowledge. And it was not only the Master she could see in this way: she saw other beings, people who had died, figures she then thought to be angels, and, when she was taken into the country, fairies and elementals and other nature spirits. Moreover this clair-

voyance seemed so natural to her, that she
was with difficulty persuaded that other people
were not endowed with the same sight.   The
sceptical laughter of her parents was painful
to her, and would have continued to be so,
had not M. H. one day when he appeared before
her, suggested that she should take no notice
of it.   Henceforward she did not speak to her
parents of what she saw, so they eventually
came to think she had grown out of "all that
foolishness," as they expressed it.   In her
eighteenth year, however, much to her surprise she discovered that her father had all of a
sudden become intensely interested in spiritism.
One of his friends had introduced him to the
subject, and from a scoffing sceptic had trans-
formed him into an almost fanatical enthusiast
This transformation prompted his daughter
once more to confide in him and let him know
that she still possessed the faculties which in
former years he had so ruthlessly derided.
The result was that he now began to look
upon her as something phenomenal and wonderful, and so deep a comradeship was en-
gendered between them that he was prepared
to give her every opportunity to further her
own development.

It was then that a romantic incident occurred.

" One evening," she told me, " my father took me to a little gathering of kindred spirits at a Mrs. Bartholomew's.   There were about twenty people there to meet a man who had, I believe you call it X-ray sight.   He could tell you how much money you had in your pockets, even if you didn't know it yourself, and things like that."

" I think I know the man," I said, " I met him myself some years ago,"   I mentioned his name.

" That's the man.   I was talking to a little group of people in a corner, when suddenly I felt as if somebody with a wonderful aura had come into the room.   I've always been able to see auras," she interpolated.   " And then a moment afterwards I saw standing in the middle of the room talking to Mrs. Bartholomew —well, you can guess who, Master M.H.   I never felt such a thrill in my life.   There at last in the flesh was the man I'd seen ever since I was a child."

" And then," I asked, tensely eager, " did he come up and speak to you ? "

" No, he had a long talk with the X-ray sight man."

" What did *you* do ?·"

" Just stayed where I was," she laughed, "far too nervous to try and get myself intro-duced."

" But of course you met him eventually ? "

"Oh, yes.   Not long afterwards Mrs. Bar-tholomew beckoned to me, introduced us and told him I was a very psychic young lady."

" Did he say anything when he saw you ? "

" He *looked*, and smiled—you know that smile of his—but he didn't say anything about having seen me before."

" Do go on," I urged, " this is intensely in-teresting.   " He must have said *something* ? "

" He did, but it wasn't to me ; he sort of talked to us both together—Mrs. Bartholomew, I mean."

" D'you know, you remind me of Madame Blavatsky," I suddenly observed.

She was taken aback.   " I hope you don't mean in looks," half laughing, " nobody could call me fat."

" No, no, I don't mean that, of course, but usedn't she to see her Master like that, and then didn't she meet him one day in the flesh ? '

"I'm afraid I don't know much *about* Madame Blavatsky."

"Well, it's of no consequence," I said, "I want to hear more about you and M.H. What happened next?"

"Mrs. Bartholomew, I think, took him off to introduce him to somebody else and after a bit I strolled into an anteroom and began to look at the books.   She had a lot of occult books there.   Nobody was in the room."

Viola then went on to tell me that he had presently come after her and taken her hand for a moment, and said: "Well, my child, we meet at last."   Afterwards he walked back to the door of her house with her, telling her a number of things about her own development. It was the greatest experience of her life—that walk back through Kensington Gardens where they rested underneath a tree facing the Round Pond, and he said "imperishable things." From that day onward, she had seen a good deal of him, and he had made friends with her father to facilitate matters, though he never took the father as an actual pupil.

"Did you find M.H. very different in those days?" I asked when she had finished.

"Only in some ways.   Haven't you noticed he's different when you get him alone from what he is when we're all together?   He hides his extraordinary love in front of his pupils *en masse*, but they all say that sometimes when he's got you to himself that sort of mask disappears. And if anyone's in trouble his compassion is simply wonderful—I've seen it, so I know . . ." After a pause: "And how the man *works !* D'you know he has only four hours' sleep every night, sometimes less."

"I didn't know it, but I'm not surprised at anything to do with *him !*"

"The curious thing is he never seems to get tired. I've often seen him sit down to a three hours' game of chess with Mr. Galais after one of the Friday night lectures."

"Which is Mr. Galais?"

"That elderly man—he's a little bald."

I nodded, recognising him from the description, then observed: "I never knew M.H. played chess. I suppose he's a splendid player?"

She looked at me knowingly. "Rather depends with whom he's playing."

I raised my eyebrows.

"He has a little habit," she explained, "of just managing to win or just managing to lose—with whomever he's playing."

We had come to the end of our lunch, and moved into the lounge for coffee and smokes.

She lit a cigarette herself and rang for cigars for me.

"By the way," I asked when comfortably settled in an armchair, "your psychic faculties—"

"Yes, what about them?"

"I thought M.H. didn't encourage that sort of thing over here."

"Neither he does as a general rule. Some of us have them all the same, but we don't proclaim it from the housetops."

"You mean you're asked not to?"

"Oh no, not that, but I know he's more pleased if we don't. He says one has to be careful not to be 'governed by vanity,' as he expresses it." She paused for a moment, then: "Perhaps you wonder why I've told *you* about them."

"Oh, I don't know about that."

"Shall I tell you why I *have* told you?"

I nodded assent.

"He suggested it himself."

"That was very nice of him," I replied, but wondered why he should have done so. "I've certainly been intensely interested in all you've told me. Just now and then, you know, I wish *I* could see again."

"Doesn't make you much happier *really*," she

said with a shrug, " it's the *feeling* side of Yoga philosophy that gives the true happiness."

" Yes.   This wonderful Bliss-Consciousness M.H. talks of—I should love to have that ! *Permanently*, I mean, for one has had touches of it."

" Yes, if one could always have *that*," she echoed regretfully.

We then turned to other subjects, and she told me *à propos* of Master's suggestion that I should be introduced to various people in Boston, that she and Miss Delafield had been putting their heads together, and the latter had suggested a tea for me at her house.   Would the following Friday suit me?   I naturally replied it *would*, having so far no engagements.   She—Miss Delafield—had further suggested that I might prefer to live in a club instead of the expensive hotel at which I was staying ; if so she could arrange to get me put up for the Arts' Club.

" Really," I said, " its very good of you both to have busied yourselves with my domestic welfare.   I should very much prefer a club. These American hotels are ruinous with the present rate of exchange."

After which I took my leave.

Miss Brind had interested me—far more than

I had ever expected.   To begin with I am always interested when I meet people with psychic faculties.   Apart from that, I discovered something very likeable about her.   With all her talents there was not a trace of self-consciousness or conceit in her character.   She had told me her experiences with a perfect simplicity of manner which I admired.   That she was a highly evolved soul I had no doubt, and would have taken her for one, even if M.H. had not told me.   But that *I*, as he had also told me, could help *her*, seemed most unlikely.   In what manner and along what lines?   Conjecture as I might I could get no nearer to any solution.   I felt that she interested me much more than I interested her.   I had not said one word of any importance during the whole time we were together.   I had played the *rôle* of a good listener, and that was all.

And then an idea suddenly struck me.   She wrote mystical books—had I perhaps to help her in some literary way?   To help her to clothe her thoughts in more poetical form, or something of that kind?   It might be so; I would ask M.H. the next time I saw him.

CHAPTER VI

PROGRESS

WHEN I got back to my hotel I found a telephone message from the Delafields asking me to dine with them that night. The message informed me that dinner was at 8 o'clock, but if I felt inclined, they begged me to come earlier; *Miss* Delafield, at any rate, would be at home after 6.30. But although I should have liked to enjoy every available moment of her society, I made a compromise and put in an appearance a little after seven. Thus we enjoyed nearly an hour's uninterrupted *tête-à-tête*, and I became more and more enmeshed in her extraordinary attractiveness.

I had had very little experience of American women before I met Clare Delafield, and hence could not tell whether the frankness of her nature was peculiar to herself or was a national characteristic. For certainly few English girls

would have permitted themselves to put into
words how much they liked a man—on such
short acquaintance—as this American girl did.
Yet she by no means gave the impression of a
flirt, but simply of a heart that was generous
with its affections, its admirations, and its enthusiasms.

" The very moment I saw you," she said—to
give an example of her candour—" I knew we
had met before and been ever such friends."

" You really felt that?" I answered, daring
to take her hand which she did not withdraw,
" I felt it too."

" Now that's just lovely," she exclaimed,
using what was evidently a habitual phrase of
hers. " But I felt it even before I met you,
now I come to think of it."

I looked at her enquiringly.

" When I read your poems," she explained.
" Ever since then I have longed to meet you—
again."

" Well, now that we have *re*-met," I said,
looking tenderly at her, " I hope we shall see a
lot of one another.

" I'm sure we shall," she replied with feeling.

We relapsed into silence for a while and both
stared meditatively into the fire.   But before

Mrs. Delafield came in, we had already taken one step towards realising our hope—we had arranged to go for a long motor-run the following day, and have lunch in the country together.

* * * * * *

It turned out to be a superb Sunday morning, and Clare called for me at eleven o'clock. We did not return before evening, and even then I was not allowed to go back to my hotel; she insisted on taking me home to supper.

That day I longed to confess my feelings, but before I dared to do so I felt it absolutely essential to find out, in as diplomatic a manner as possible, her views on marriage. Supposing she entertained hopes in that direction—what then? It is true I was nearly twenty years her senior, yet I hardly looked a day over forty. That being so, I inclined to the idea that the difference in our ages would not of necessity strike her as an obstacle—if she had any matrimonial intentions. But although it proved to be a difficult piece of conversational manœuvering, I accomplished it in the end, and made the comforting discovery that she was as chary of entering the bonds of martimony as I was myself. Firstly she and her Mamma, as she called her—with the accent on the first syllable—were "all in all" to each other, and she felt that to marry and leave her would be extremely selfish; secondly she informed me that none of her three brothers were happily married, and, therefore, she had very good reasons for not regarding the conjugal state as an enviable one.

The ground was therefore cleared after these avowals on her part; nevertheless I restrained myself and postponed the moment when I should actually tell her what I felt for her. Not that I imagined she was unaware of this—I had that day given her many signs—but I thought that any undue haste on my part to bring matters to a climax would be inartistic. It was enough that we had made headway towards what prospected to be a very absorbing and inspiring romance; and one moreover which, as I came later on to know, bore a highly occult significance. Indeed it is for that reason only that I include it in this book, for it has an indirect bearing on him who was now a Master to us both.

The tea which Clare and her mother gave "in my honour" was one of those unsatisfactory American functions at which one shakes hands with a number of people, and nothing much further happens—at least not in proportion to the outlay, if I can so express myself. There must have been fifty people present, including many professors from the University, yet at the end of it all I saw no prospect of making a single friend as the result. But as it turned out later, I was not altogether correct in my surmise, as in the course of time I was invited to a good many dinners, to which Claire was also invited.

Of the Master I had seen nothing since the Friday on which we had taken the drive together. He had on the following day gone to New York, but was to return on Wednesday for the lecture. When, however, we arrived at his house that evening one of the *chelas* announced that a telephone message had been received saying that he would be late. We therefore had to amuse ourselves for nearly three quarters of an hour with general conversation before he put in an appearance. But as Claire was now enrolled among the pupils and had come to attend her first lecture, the time by no means hung heavy on my hands. My only regret was that a shorter lecture was likely to be the result of the delay.

When M.H. finally arrived he apologised for keeping us waiting, but said he had been detained; after which he stepped on to the little platform and began the discourse I have headed 'The Philosophy of Humour."

The Philosophy of Humour.

"In some of the books on Yoga mention is made of the seven austerities, and one of these austerities is *cheerfulness*. It may seem strange to the uninitiated that such a thing as cheerfulness can be regarded as an austerity, so I think we might employ ourselves to advantage this evening by looking into the matter a little more closely.

Now continuous cheerfulness has unquestionably to do with the will ; that is to say, *it can be induced* if we only take the trouble to make the necessary effort.   I notice, however, that many students of occultism, far from taking that trouble, exert themselves to produce exactly the opposite effect, and for reasons best known to themselves 'pull the long face,' as it is called, and dress in garments remotely suggesting 'sack-cloth and ashes.'   These good people are labouring under some pietistic delusion that what you women call dowdiness has some connection with spirituality, whereas in truth it is but vanity in disguise. Such people of course are merely taking themselves too seriously ; they think that because they chance to know a little about Karma, Masters, Reincarnation and Immortality, they must contrive to let their poor ordinary fellows see that there is some difference between themselves and these poor ordinary fellows. But that difference, if paraded at all, should be one of joy and not of sorrow. Oh, I assure you," he added, " we Masters are not at all flattered to think that people must go into mourning because they have heard of our existence and all that we stand for."

This was greeted with loud laughter.

" It reminds me of the child I once heard of who asked his mother if *clergymen* wore black because they were always thinking about death . . . Perhaps that really *is* the reason only they don't know it."

M. H. lit a cigar and puffed at it meditatively for a few moments. Then he proceeded :

" Now hand in hand with cheerfulness goes another very useful quality—that is a sense of humour. It is precisely through this sense of humour that we are prevented from falling into the error I've just mentioned ; I mean this tendency to take ourselves too seriously. We ought in fact to be able to see a humorous side to everything, I don't care what it is, though by that I do not imply that we should have no self-control and should burst out laughing on all occasions. If we *could* see the humorous side of everything, whether we show it outwardly or

not, I can assure you that we would not act in
the foolish way we so often do. It happens, as
you know, to be a curious irony of fate that the
very people who are lacking in this humoristic
sense are the very ones who prove so irresistibly
humorous to others. They are much like
drunkards who, not being able to see their own
actions, usually behave in a way which makes
everyhody else laugh. I often think if these
long-face-pulling persons could see themselves
as we Masters can see them they too might be
induced to laugh *with* us—which would be their
salvation.

Not long ago I had my eye on a prospective
pupil who had recently taken up the Higher
Occultism with most laudable and unusual zest.
She had previously been a happy, light-hearted
creature full of gaiety and humour, sane in mind
and healthy in body, and on that account was
especially popular among her friends. Well, as
I said, she took up occultism and the first result
was that she changed completely. She lost all
her light-heartedness, lost her interest in her
friends, began to neglect her appearance, ceased
to be witty and amusing—in short she became
a most zealous member of the ‘ Long-faced
League.’ ”

A ripple of laughter went through the assembly.
" Finally I contrived that she should be
brought to me. She arrived one day, trembling
with nervousness, as if she imagined I was an
acrimonious tribal chief, little short of Jehovah
himself. Of course the first thing I did was to
make a joke—just to relieve the intensity of the
atmosphere! Why you should laugh before
you know what the joke was," he interpolated
in reponse to the renewed ripple, " I can't
think . . . However you certainly never *will*
know that joke, as I've forgotten it myself.
All the same, good or bad, its effect was
startling—my visitor nearly fainted. A Master
make a joke! This was something quite un-
heard-of in her occult philosophy! She had
been taught to believe that Masters were glori-
fied prigs—and she was actually disappointed
to discover they were not. Well, in the end I
sent her away with the injunction not to read
one occult book for six months, but to confine
herself entirely to Bernard Shaw, Chesterton,
and any other witty and sparkling writers she
could find. As to seeing me again, of this I
made no mention, but I told a *Chela* to drop
her the hint that the ways of Masters, though
often mysterious, were not as unreasonable

as she might suppose. Let her exercise patience and faith and await events. Fortunately—though after a good deal of soul-disturbance, resulting from her disillusionment —her faith, which was considerable, triumphed, and in a year's time I saw her again and she became a pupil. Since then, she has learnt to acquire, or better said, to re-aquire, the divine quality of cheerfulness."

The Master paused for a moment.

"But apart from the inconsistency of it all, you must see what harm this long-face-pulling policy can do to the cause of occultism. Remember, you do not tread the Path solely for your own benefit—you tread it for the benefit of *all*. Yet what inducement, I should like to know, do you offer others to study occultism, if the only perceptible effect it has on you is to make you a morose, crankish, and entirely undesirable member of society? How would you treat a man who came to you and said : 'I've got hold of a most wonderful philosophy and I want you to study it too—it possesses the incomparable faculty of making one thoroughly miserable?'

"And now to the next point. What use can we make of humour in connection with the

overcoming of our unworthy desires and
weaknesses? If we only take the trouble to
reflect, we can do much along this line, both
for ourselves and for others. A *Chela* once
wrote a book in which he very eloquently
showed that all human weaknesses, jealousy,
pride, anger and so forth were simply childish ;
and that is absolutely true. (I strongly advise
you to read that book ; it is called ' The Way
of the Childish '* by Shri Advaitacharya). But
we can go a step further and say that all human
weaknesses are *ridiculous ;* for that is equally
true. You have, however, to learn the art of
seeing them as such, instead of being swept up
in the delusion that they're necessary and even
dignified. To give a very simple example :
there's a type of person, generally a woman,
whom one describes as touchy ; she is always
getting offended over this or that triviality.
You meet her one day and she greets you with
a long face or puts on a haughty air and you
can't make out what is the matter with her.
And then after quite a long time you discover
that you hadn't called on her when she thought
you ought to have, or you had been guilty of
some equally trifling sin of omission. And all

* Kegan Paul, London.

the time she has been taking a vast amount of
trouble to keep up a grievance against you and
to pull that face whenever she thinks of you or
happens to meet you in the street; perhaps
she even cuts you altogether for a while.   But
what lies at the root of the whole matter?   A
lack of the humoristic sense, of course.   This
good woman cannot realise that she is simply
being ridiculous; she imagines she is standing
on her dignity or teaching you a wonderful
lesson in this roundabout way.   That she is
merely teaching you that she herself is a verv
foolish person, never occurs to her.

So there you have one example of what I
mean.   Contrive to awaken a useful sense of
humour in a woman like that and you may cure
her.   After all she is only suffering from an
illusion.   And it's the same in connection with
every sort of weakness, if we are only prepared to
carry our analysis far enough—for it *is* a question
of analysis.   Take up one of your weaknesses
and really dissect it; try to see its why and
wherefore, and if you are fearless and honest
enough to get down to bedrock you'll discover
the whole matter is merely foolishness.   Say
you are in love with someone, and you are
always wanting to embrace them and touch them

and are unhappy unless you're doing this continually ; you may even weep because you can't
be forever indulging yourself in this way, for
your desire is so strong. Well, now, analyse
that desire and see what it really amounts to.
Here are you in this world with its thousands
of enjoyments and its thousands of beautiful
things, the sky, the sea, sunshine, flowers and
singing birds, its artistic beauties in the shape
of pictures, music, poetry, books and architect-
ure ; its human beauties in the shape of millions
of people who could afford you an endless source
of delight if you only adopted the right attitude
towards them. Yet in the face of these wonderful things what are you doing ? You're sighing
and moaning just because you can't touch a few
inches or a few feet of ordinary common or
garden human skin. It may even be rough and
hairy but that doesn't affect you, because it just
happens to belong to one particular person out
of all the millions in the universe. Now I ask
you, don't you think you're being rather ridiculous ? Aren't you making a great fuss about
very little ? Why should your whole happiness
depend on putting your two inches of mouth
against another person's two inches of mouth ?
Surely your sense of proportion must have

evaporated.   You laugh—but I'm expressing it
in this crude form on purpose.   We're trying to
see the matter entirely denuded of all glamour.
As long as you only look at it through an atmosphere of roses and perfumes you ll not get
to the bedrock of actuality.   But sweep all these
away and get down to hard dry facts and then
see how you stand.   That is the way to recover
your sense of proportion, and to re-awaken your
sanity and sense of humour.   It's just the latter
which acts as the balance wheel of our characters.
Do you suppose a lunatic could imagine himself
to be Jesus Christ or the King of England if he
hadn't lost his sense of humour together with
his sense of actuality ?   One would suppose he
need only look down at his own legs to see that
he's thinking nonsense.   Did Jesus Christ ever
wear a pair of trousers ?   I suppose I really
oughtn't to ask such a question," the Master
interpolated with one of his characteristic smiles,
" some people would think it irreverent, but
that's because, as Bernard Shaw very aptly puts
it, they don't regard Jesus Christ as a reality ;
if they did they might be induced to apply His
teachings a good deal more than they normally do.
   We *must* cultivate our sense of humour
together with an uninterrupted cheerfulness of

mind ; otherwise we shall not acquire wisdom.
God *has* given this power to all of us if we
only choose to use it.   Potentially it's there, but
you must bring it into manifestation.   If you
had three legs instead of two what would be the
good of them if you didn't learn how to use
them ?   Practice is everything ; you practice to
acquire facility in this, that and the other art ;
but not one of these will repay you to the extent
that the practice of joyousness will repay you.
Tell yourselves repeatedly : ' All is joy.'   Fall
asleep with that phrase in your mind last thing
at night, and let it be your first waking thought
in the morning.   Then one day it will begin to
work subconsciously, and you'll retain that joy
as a permanent consciousness.   Has it ever occurred to you to ask yourselves why some of
you find it so difficult to be unselfish ?   It is
solely because you have not properly caught
hold of this feeling of joy.   You dislike doing
a quantity of unselfish things because they bore
and worry you.   But if you were always conscious of joy do you suppose anything in the
universe could bore you ?   *Therefore seek ye
first the kingdom of Joy*—which is an attribute
of God—*and all things shall be added unto you*—
even unselfishness ! "

CHAPTER VII

LOVE AND INSPIRATION

AFTER the discourse that evening I walked home with Clare. "Well, what do you think of it all?" I asked her when we had got outside.

"Wonderful, but not in the least what I expected. My! He's so cunningly humorous. I never associated philosophy and religion with humour before."

"Or calling a spade a spade," I added.

"No, that's something new to me, too."

"You weren't shocked?" I threw in tentatively.

"Not a *little* bit," she said with conviction, "still, I can't quite look at love in the way *he* does, can you?"

"You mean the few inches of human skin?"

"M'm . . ." with a nod.

"He doesn't look at it like that himself. I've heard him talk very differently."

"Then why did he say that?"

"As far as I can gather—merely from what I know of him, of course—because he wants us to see things from every point of view. But I've heard him say that some people can evolve more quickly through falling in love than through any other means."

She suddenly looked at me with joy in her eyes, as a child looks when you tell it a treat is in store. "You've really heard him say *that?*" she said.

"Yes, really."

"What a relief!" she sighed humorously. "There are some ideals I wouldn't have shattered for anything."

"I don't think you need be afraid," I soothed her, "you've no idea how understanding he is. Do you know what he said to me the day I had lunch with you?"

"Tell me."

"That romances were necessary to poets, because they assist inspiration."

"How lovely of him! But . . . do you have so *many*, then?"

"Depends what you *call* many; it's quite time since I had one—until——"

"Until what?"

"Until I came over here."

"You mean—you've gotten one now?" she asked hurriedly.

"I should *like* to have one, but—well, it takes two to make a romance, doesn't it?"

She was silent, looking as if she did not know what to say; so I took her arm and insinuated my hand into hers. "Tell me," I asked, laughing, "are you really a little dense, or only pretending to be?"

She put her head on one side and glanced at me with a playful expression. "Perhaps a little of both," she answered; then after a pause: "There are some things a woman likes to hear—*said*. . . ."

"Then I'll say them," I replied; and did so!

*　　*　　*　　*　　*　　*

I had, before seeing Clare home, made an appointment to lunch with M.H. the following day. Viola Brind had also been invited, but I was to be at his house half an hour before lunch time, so as to have a private chat before she arrived. I found him with Arkwright, but the latter, after saying a few pleasantries, took his departure.

"Well," said M.H. genially, "you look extra happy this morning."

" I am," I answered, laughing.

"Things been going well with you in Boston?"

" Extremely well ; so well that I had quite a bad night."

" Sounds paradoxical."

" When one's thoughts are unusually pleasant one hardly likes to leave them and sink into unconsciousness.

" Oh, I see."

" I wonder *you* ever sleep at all."

" Why shouldn't I ? "

" For the same reason, only more so. If I had your perpetual feeling of bliss, I'm sure I should never want to lose it by going to sleep."

He smiled indulgently at me. " But I don't lose it; I merely lose consciousness of my body."

" Fool ! " I exclaimed, tapping my forehead, " when will I fully grasp this idea of the *unconditional ?* "

" You'll grasp it one day, if———"

" I carry out your program," I finished, guessing what was in his mind.

He nodded assent, but immediately changed the conversation. " You have seen Viola Brind ? "

" I had a most interesting lunch with her. She told me all about her meeting with you."

"Ah, she did, did she?" with one of his whimsical expressions, "so you're getting along well together?"

"Oh, I think so—quite.   She certainly seems a most unusual girl."

"She *is*."

"Tell me," I said, suddenly remembering the question I had intended to ask him, "is it with her books you thought perhaps I could help her?"

"Well, yes—partly," the answer did not sound very convincing, so I was still mystified ; and as again he changed the conversation I felt he did not wish me to pursue the subject.   "And Miss Delafield, you have seen her?" he asked.

"I've more than seen her, I've fallen in love with her," I said, feeling a trifle embarrassed, "I hope you don't think that at *my* age——"

"It's *infra dig*," he supplied with a twinkle, "on the contrary, it shows that the heart's still young.   If we tread the Path, my son, it's necessary to retain this youthfulness of heart.   Besides what avail to censure any of our pupils for falling in love, however old?   The karma that is to be *must* be."

"All the same," he continued earnestly, "they should use discrimination and not allow their romances to lure them from their work or from the projects their Masters may have in view for them.   In your case remember that your artistic activities must always come first, for these are for the world's sake.   You write to *teach* humanity, and to give to humanity higher and nobler ideals.   Never forget that.   And especially do not forget it whilst in the throes of a romance, but let the extra love and joy which in such circumstances you feel, act as inspiration.   And as I write this, my memory harks back to a fragment of one of J. M. H.'s talks to us all, dealing with how the karma of even an unconventional love-affair can in certain circumstances be made to yield its lesson—especially to the woman.   And I cite it here because it explains still further why J. M. H. never actually interfered with the course of our romance.

He had said in the talk referred to: Most women when they love are not prepared to give something for nothing.   They are not prepared to sink their pride without asking for anything in return: they usually hope to possess the man himself in marriage, at any rate ultimately, if not at once.   But think how you can elevate a woman if you can bring her to give love to a man not for her own sake but for the world's sake; that through her giving he may receive inspiration, and through that inspiration Humanity may be richer.   Don't you see that in this way you can further that woman's spiritual development almost more than by any other method—I mean through the great renunciation you will thus be teaching her? And supposing the uncharitable and short-sighted world does cast aspersions upon her, and calls her harsh but unmerited names—is it not worth it? For if this happens, she will also learn heroism and indifference to the calumny of the conventional-minded. But to return from my digression. Although J. M. H. naturally did not suggest that I should actually ask for Clare's or any other woman's love for the purpose of enhancing literary inspiration, he did proceed to remind me that only those who understand the nature of woman to the very core, can fully appreciate the joy she experiences when told by the man she loves that she inspires him to greater work.

There was a knock at the door and Viola Brind entered. She was fashionably dressed in a manner which showed off her elegant little figure to advantage, and at that moment I felt I liked her in a friendly brotherly sort of way even more than I had done hitherto.

"Well, Viola," said M. H. giving her an affectionate pat on the shoulder, "we're going to have a cosy little lunch *à trois*. Hope you're

hungry ?   Swami Vivekananda used to say the
first sign of true religion is a good sound
appetite.   If the heart is at peace the appetite
is good."

She laughed by way of answer and then
shook hands with me.

M.H. went into the hall and we heard him
shouting in Italian : " Alberto, is lunch ready ? "

" *Si, Signor*," came the response : then he
reappeared and asked us to come into the
dining-room.

The Master's lunches were an achievement
of daintiness and lavishness combined.   The
variety of fruits spread out on the table provided
a most picturesque sight.   There were large
bunches of grapes, oranges, apples, bananas,
pomegranates and grape-fruit, together with
nuts of various sorts.   First we were served with
oeufs à la crème, then with a cooked nut-food
accompanied by an assortment of vegetables.
After that appeared a most delicious chocolate
cake covered with whipped cream, followed by
cheese and biscuits with celery.   Finally we
attacked the large variety of fruits.

During this meal M.H. entertained us with
anecdotes interspersed with bits of wisdom ; he
also commented on international politics and the

occult meaning of revolutions; on the strange
trend of modern painting, and on many other
topics of the day.   And all this with at times
an almost child-like charm of manner, and witti-
cisms which evoked many outbursts of laughter
from both Viola Brind and myself.   This lunch-
party in fact was one of the most enjoyable
hours I had spent for many years; and as we
got up from the table I felt more than ever
struck by the extraordinary variety of powers
which my Master possessed, and the rapidity
with which he could change from one mood—
I might almost say from one *personality*—to
another.   When I thought back to all that he
had said to me but a short while before, and
how especially at that moment I had felt him
to be well-nigh patriarchal in his wisdom, I
could hardly believe him to be the same
person.

To quote an instance of this, as we sat over
our coffee and cigars I said to him :   "What I
don't understand about people who have clairvoyant faculties, and so I suppose know everything' already, is that they ever need to ask
questions."

They both laughed, and Viola said to M.H.,
"I leave *you* to explain that."

" Lazy creature," he teased her, " I'm always left to do all the work."

Nevertheless he told me what I wanted to know in the most natural way. " People with clairvoyant faculties are as human as anybody else. After all, because they may know a good many things about you, it would be rather dull if they sat there like deaf-mutes and never gave the impression that they took an atom of interest in any of your doings. It's *your* feelings they're considering when they ask questions. Suppose Viola and I had gone to a concert last night and you'd met her early this morning and she'd said: 'M.H. and I did enjoy that concert,' that wouldn't prevent you from saying the next time you saw me : ' Well, how was the concert ?'—now would it? After all, as long as we live in this world, we must adapt ourselves at any rate to most of its customs. It may not matter to me personally whether I'm talking or keeping silent or even breaking stones in the road, but it may matter very considerably to my acquaintances. Besides, although you who are initiated may understand my peculiar ways, there are a great many who would be highly astonished if, on meeting them, I proceeded to *tell* them everything about themselves, instead of to *ask* them.   It's all very well for a character in a story-book like Sherlock Holmes—but in real life one mustn't do these things.   It wouldn't be ethical to show off like that."

"What I admire so enormously in you," I said, "is that you're always willing to explain yourself instead of making a mystery of things."

"There *is* no mystery," he declared, "it's not *we* who make the mystery about ourselves, it's other people.   Some persons have a mania for mystery-making, and *we* are their unfortunate victims.   Because a thing is hidden, it is not of necessity mysterious.   X-rays are hidden, but that doesn't make them secret and occult.   All together the word occult is not a happy one, but since it *has* come into use, it's very difficult to get rid of now.   Of course there are certain things we can't tell to every Tom, Dick, and Harry because they'd misuse their powers and hurt themselves and others.   Look how people injured themselves when they first started using the X-rays; but X-rays are comparatively harmless beside some of the so-called occult forces. We *must* keep them secret from the world at large because we dare not take the responsibility of revealing them.   But that's all there is to it. You can't——"

We were interrupted by Alberto who came to say that the motor was at the door.

"By the way," said M.H., getting up from his chair, "if it's a nice day on Sunday week we might take a run into the country. What do you say? Next Sunday I'm not free, but the following one——"

We said we'd be delighted.

"And now I'm afraid I must go."

I walked with Viola Brind as far as her door, and then went to have tea with Clare—and with a clear conscience. . . .

CHAPTER VIII

EGOTISM

By the following Saturday I had moved into the Arts' Club, and as it was permitted to invite ladies, I asked Viola Brind to dine with me that evening. The result was a marked degree of progress towards that friendship which the Master desired should exist between us, though we were both still ignorant as to what its motive might be. She confessed that he had told her to cultivate *me*, and I gathered had done so in almost the same words as he had told me to cultivate *her*—namely with the idea of mutual help; but she too had been left in the dark as to the nature of that help.

"I can understand that *you* with your extraordinary poetic talents," she said, "could help *me*, but how *I* could help *you*—I really can't think."

"The very same thing I thought about *you*,"

I laughed. "With *your* psychic powers you can help *me;* but although I might be able to give you a literary hint here and there—it would be so slight as to be almost negligible."

" Master says your modesty is phenomenal," she teased me.

" I think we'd better change the subject!" I laughed, and proceeded to talk about the lecture of the previous Wednesday and its allusion to human love. From that I was able to glide into the subject of my own romantic feelings for Clare. Not that I especially wanted to confide in Viola Brind at that moment, but I knew that nothing cements friendship so quickly as an exchange of confidences. And my confession did result in an exchange : after listening to me sympathetically for a while she then made a romantic confession of her own. She told me that for some years she had been in love with a man over in England. This man had selfishly played with her feelings—because, I take it, they flattered his vanity—and at the same time had conducted a number of other affairs about which he quite unblushingly took Viola into his confidence. She on her part had accepted these confidences and nobly sympathised with the man, the reason, as she expressed it, being that she preferred to have his friendship than nothing at all.

"One thing at any rate I learnt," she told me, "and that was to overcome jealousy."

She was still in the throes of this unfortunate affair when M.H. wrote to her telling her to come to America. She found it a terrible wrench—leaving this man—but the prospect of being with her Master outweighed all other considerations. Moreover she realised that through separation she might eventually come to *forget;* and her own father who knew of her unhappiness and its cause was only too ready to assist her in the process. When she told him of the Master's letter and the project it contained he furnished the money and packed her off to Boston without delay.

Naturally after she had related all this I asked if the separation had had the desired effect.

"Partially, yes," was her answer. "I still love the man, but I'm no longer unhappy. Master has taught me how to get over my unhappiness. There is a way, you know. There are even several ways as far as that goes—it's a question of finding the particular one best suited to your own temperament. Not that *you* need one," she added with a smile, "but you

never know.   As M.H. so often reminds us
' it's best to make hay while the sun shines.' "

As I saw her into her taxi I said with an
affectionate little pressure of her hand   We
are friends, aren't we ? "

" Excellent ones," she answered.

                *   *   *   *

During the following days I saw nothing of
M.H. ; he was too busy to give me an appointment, but on the Wednesday I of course attended
the evening lecture.   I had had an early dinner
with Clare and her mother, and so had escorted
the former to the Master's house.

As M.H. was about to step on to the little
platform to give his discourse he casually took
up a book which one of the students had left
on the table with cigars and a carafe of water
placed by the Master's chair.

" Aha—' The Egoist ' by Meredith," he observed, turning over a few pages.   " Well, there
are plenty of those walking about . . . ' Rogue
in Porcelain '—I remember the thing ; I read it
just after it came out.   Once I had a short
philosophical conversation with Meredith.   He
had a very fine type of mind, and incidentally a
very fine face."

He put the book back on the table and sat down.

" I think we might do worse than take up the subject of egotism this evening," he said, " and see how it looks under the philosophical microscope, and what lies at the root of it.   It's not a happy characteristic in its acute form, because it implies a limitation of consciousness instead of an expansion ; but I don't intend to deal with it in its acute form—that would be rather too obvious to need discussing—but in its subtler form, the form we call egotism in contradistinction to ordinary undisguised selfishness.   Now to begin with, what do we really mean by egotism ?   Not ordinary hit-you-in-the-eye sort of conceit—but something a little less crude than that.   It is more that taking-of-oneself-and-one's-work-too-seriously attitude which, I think, partly arises from an insufficient all-round sense of humour.   Persons troubled with this complaint seem utterly unable to get away from the subject of their work ; they are like a certain type of amateur—or even professional—pianist who can't keep from the piano, and must always be strumming even if nobody wants to listen. And mind you—for let us be fair—it is not only artists who are afflicted in this way.   I have

known writers on mystical subjects, theosophists,
occultists, politicians, social workers, scientists—
it matters not—who all exhibit this characteristic ; they are not conscious of it, but their acquaintances are, and in consequence soon begin
to get bored with them. 'Always the same old
subject!' these acquaintances think, 'if only to
God they'd shut up just for once in a while or
talk about something else!' And it is not only
their acquaintances who think like this but also
those who read their works if they be writers,
as in the case of some mystics I have just
mentioned. However elevated the subject, this
egotism peeps through between the lines. These
writers seem to be obsessed by the word
'sacredness'—the sacredness of what they are
writing about and particularly of their own
mission. They would think it unseemly to make
a joke about that mission, so they write and talk
with bated breath, and metaphorically, if not
actually, fold their hands and look up to heaven
with a rapt expression of countenance. There
is one woman I know who has got so much into
the habit of this that even in ordinary conversation she talks as if she were saying her prayers.
She's a fine soul and one of our pupils, but
she'll have to acquire a good deal more sense

of humour before she can hope to reach
Adeptship.

" And now, what is the explanation of it all ?
Well—it is a stage; a stage on the journey most
souls have to travel ; it is a milestone on the
road of concentration.   Let us examine this
statement a little more closely.   When concentration has not been perfectly mastered, you find
you can concentrate on certain things but not on
others.   Some people find it easier to concentrate on the tip of their nose than on an abstract
idea, and *vice versa*.   But note this—only when
you are able to concentrate on *any*thing you wish,
have you fully mastered concentration.   There
is a restricted type of concentration such as
when you sit down for five minutes and practise
holding the thoughts to one idea, and there is,
as it were, an unrestricted type ; and by that I
mean when an idea or cause is ever-present at
the back of your minds for years in succession.
You get a temporary form of this when you are
in love.   You do not sit down and deliberately
concentrate on your beloved, yet you are thinking of him or her practically all the time.   And
that is good in its way ; as you know, I never
discourage any of you from falling in love, just
because I do realise, among many other things,

how good it is from a concentrational point of view. This is however by the way. What we are at present concerned with is this concentration on some cause or idea which not only may last a life-time, but which colours almost every moment of that life as well. Look at your own selves: the higher philosophy, Occultism or the Science of Yoga—the name doesn't matter—is so incessantly in your minds that it permeates all your activities, all your emotions and all your thoughts. And that is concentration of a very powerful kind, yet it is not perfect concentration. And why? Because if you cannot switch it off when circumstances demand that you should do so, you have not learnt *complete* mastery over the mind. For there is such a thing as concentration minus wisdom. I once knew a man who had such perfect concentration that if you shot off a pistol in his presence, he never stirred. This man was not an occultist: he was a Professor, and took no interest in occult matters. But he would nevertheless sit in front of the fire and go off into such a state of abstraction that nothing could rouse him but a thorough good shaking. And yet astonishing and laudable as his concentrative faculties were, he had not complete control of his mind: one day he appeared at a dinner-party in his dress coat and a khaki-coloured pair of trousers—he had concentrated his mind on the upper portion of his body, but had left his legs to take care of themselves.

"There are again people who are so concentrated on their own thoughts that when in a train they'll pass the station at which they ought to get out. That is another form of injudicious concentration, or incomplete mastery over the mind. If you can't help becoming concentrated whenever you think at all, that is not a blessing but rather a curse. The ideal state is when a man can say : 'I've a quarter of an hour before I get to my station ; for exactly that space of time I will concentrate, and not a moment longer.'

"Such then are the pitfalls of restricted concentration, but of the larger concentration permeating a life-time Egotism is the pitfall.

"Now we have exhibited the disease, but what is the remedy ? Are we to throw cold water on our enthusiasms and think less of the Cause, whatever it may be ? No, for that would be a step backwards instead of forwards. We must temper our enthusiasm with wisdom, and for one thing learn the very valuable lesson that seriousness and humour are not enemies but the very closest of allies. Let us take a very trite example : I am obliged to travel to Chicago ; I therefore buy the necessary ticket and proceed on my way. It stands to reason that I take that journey seriously, otherwise instead of making for the station at the proper time, I should be dawdling about, or doing things calculated to make me miss that train. But having once got comfortably settled in my seat, am I to talk of nothing except that I *am* in the train ; that I *am* on my way to Chicago : and am I to pull a long face and not make a single joke about trains, travelling, or even Chicago itself, or the reason I have for going there ? Surely that wouldn't be the behaviour of a reasonable being. Besides what else might it not denote? A highly disturbed state of the nervous system. It is quite right to take a thing seriously, but it is not wisdom to be too serious in the taking of it, paradoxical though the statement may sound.

"Still, this paradox is just what you must learn in connection with your art, your occultism, your mission, or any all-important cause you may have at heart. But there is another and even greater lesson you need to learn ere you can reach the goal. Our philosophy has taught you there is only *one* Life, *one* Consciousness. That being so, that One life permeates everything and consequently every one of your little selves. Thus you are dependent on that One Life for every atom of energy you possess and hence for all your actions. Very well then : say you create a work of art ; are you as Mr. or Miss X. creating that work of art, or is the One Life, Brahman, or God creating it through you ? Therein lies the whole crux of the matter, and that is just what you forget. Suppose for instance you write a book, but a friend gives you all the ideas for that book, are you going to take the full credit to yourself and leave his name out altogether ? If you're a mean, ungrateful sort of creature, yes—but surely not otherwise. Can you with honesty say you've written that book at all ? Oh, I grant your hand has written it, but what is that ? And so you see that egotism arises from Maya—the illusion that it is ' I ' who perform actions, ' I ' who produce ideas, ' I ' who invent plots, when all the time it is God Who does these things through you. Whence do you take the energy to live at all ? From the All-Life. Whence do you take the substance to build your body? From the All-Substance. Whence do you take the air you breath ? From the one common

stock of air. Whence do you take your ideas?
From the One Mind—and so it goes on. And
you don't even *ask* for those ideas : you just take
them and call them yours, or at any rate *behave*
as if you called them yours ; and that is egotism.

"But perhaps you'll object and say: 'This is
all a quibble; whether I admit or deny your
assertion, it can't make any real difference.'
But my answer to that is 'the proof of the
pudding is in the eating.' Admit my assertion
and manifest its truth in your lives, and you are
lovable, admirable human beings ; deny my assertion and fail to manifest its truth, and you
are unlovable, unadmirable, egotistical bores.
Oh, I'm willing to go with you this far and
concede that it's not so much the Truth itself
that matters but the effect of the realisation of
that Truth upon yourselves Once you have
succeeded in banishing Maya in the shape of
egotism from your characters, there is no
necessity to be muttering the truth to yourselves at every step you take A man mistakes
a piece of rope for a snake, then realises it is
only a rope after all : that doesn't mean to say
that for the rest of his life, whenever he chances
upon a bit of rope, he has to repeat to himself:
'This is not a snake, this is not a snake!' Once

realise the truth, 'and the truth shall make you free.' This being the case, you will find there are a number of great men, be they artists or others, who are '*born* modest.' They are old souls and have learnt the lesson in a previous life. It does not matter whether they remember *how* they learnt it—can you even remember exactly *how*, when and where you learnt your alphabets?—the important fact is that the lesson *has* been learnt."

The Master lit a cigar, reflected for a moment, then proceeded :

"There is a form of egotism which is so insidious as to appear to be its own antithesis, and it is one we must, for that reason, specially guard against. It is usually connected with love—I don't mean *necessarily* sex-love, but affection of a more or less intense kind. As with all egotism, it involves selfishness and vanity, but both of these are very effectually disguised, and unless we penetrate deep, will not be perceptible at all. Let me give an example: a woman has a friend, say of the same sex, whom she idolizes. She spends her time doing everything she can think of for that friend, from giving her chocolates and flowers, making her pretty underclothes, running end-

less messages, darning her stockings, to—well,
helping her to wash her hair. Some of those
who look on at these manifestations exclaim :
'Dear me, what devotion! How touching!
How beautiful! Such love—such unselfishness!' But is it such unselfishness? When
this ultra-devoted girl hears of somebody else
giving her friend chocolates or what not, is she
quite happy, does she feel quite at ease? She
has an uncomfortable sensation which she cannot define, but which upsets her equilibrium and
takes some of the sunshine out of her life.
Somehow she feels that other people's chocolates oughtn't to taste quite as sweet as *her*
chocolates; that other people's message-running
oughtn't to be so effectual as *her* message-
running ; that other people's shampoo-powders
oughtn't to be as cleansing and sweet-smelling
as *her* shampoo-powders, and so forth. Then
let us suppose an invisible somebody argues
with her : 'But don't you want your friend to
be happy?' She answers passionately : 'Why,
the whole day long I'm doing nothing else but
trying to make her happy—I'd even die for her
happiness.' Then says the voice: 'If that's the
case, why are you upset when she *is* happy?'
Silence—no reply.

"What is the explanation? All that unselfish
ness is only pseudo-unselfishness—it is disguised
egotism.   As long as this ultra-devoted girl can
herself be the giver of happiness to her friend
all is joy, but as soon as anybody else gives that
happiness misery is the result.   Just as vanity
is really the cause of jealousy, so in this case is
vanity also the cause of wanting to be the sole
giver.   And needless to say wherever there is
vanity there is egotism, since the latter is an
attribute of the former.   You have heard it said
that blessed is he who gives cheerfully : but
sometimes it would be more fitting to say blessed
is he who cheerfully allows *others* to give.
What should it matter to us how happiness
comes to those we love ? The chief thing is
that they *are* happy.   There's a lot of this
pseudo-unselfishness and pseudo-selfish love in
the world ; you see it in various kinds of relationships, between mothers and sons, mothers
and daughters, wives and husbands, and more
than often between sweethearts.   There is a
certain species of demonstrative lover who shows
it up to perfection.   He is ready to die for you,
as he says, twenty times a day, but when he is
not—theoretically—dying for you he can't *live*
without you.   He's forever telling you how

much he adores you, and how it *is* impossible for him to live without you even for a moment, let alone a lifetime. Oh, I assure you his intentions are honourable with a vengeance : he is out either for marriage or suicide. Truly he's a marvellous lover : never have you felt so loved and so *needed* by anybody in the world before. The love-language that pours from his lips sends you into the seventh heaven ; you hear that everything about you is absolute perfection—everything. It's wonderful to find a being who really appreciates **you,** wonderful to be *wanted* like that."

The Master paused, then altered his inflection. " Well, and granted it is wonderful, so are the first dreams of the opium-eater—ecstatic, glorious ; but how about the drawbacks which come later ? You begin to find that to be so intensely wanted is not entirely honied sweetness after all. You begin to find yourself inconveniently tied ; when you want to go for a walk your husband prefers to stay at home and make love to you. When he has to go on a business-journey to an unattractive place he insists on taking you with him, even though the train tires you. When you want to ask some friend for the evening he prefers to be alone with you. Eventually you

find that neither your body nor your soul are
your own any more, and come to the horrifying
conclusion that this once immaculate pattern of
all lovers is a most selfish and impossible
husband. And unfortunately you are right.
Was he really loving *you* all that time? No—
he was loving himself—what you could give
him—*his* enjoyment. He was solely concerned
with what he could get, and all his fine phrases
were nothing but selfish pleadings in disguise.
If you had thwarted him he would have been
ready to die—not *for* you, but *because* of you.
The blow to his vanity, combined with the frus-
tration of his desires, would have been too much
for him, so he would have sought peace in
suicide. He is the egoist *par excellence* who
would far prefer not to *be* than not to *have*.
And there are thousands like him, with minor
variations. What does that seemingly poetic
phrase 'to die of a broken heart' really mean?
To die of selfishness; the heart simply goes to
pieces under the strain of incessant wanting
what it can't have . . .

"I have now said enough to show you how
insidious are selfishness and egotism, and how
the latter, like a worm, may wriggle itself into
all the holes and crevices of our characters, only

to peep out its head in places we least expect.
Guard against that reptile : he is not beautiful ;
he is a disfiguring parasite to be destroyed by
the purifying antiseptic of Wisdom."

CHAPTER IX

THE ARKWRIGHTS

A DAY or two later I went to tea at the Arkwrights'—for there *was* a Mrs. Arkwright,
though I have not mentioned her hitherto.
She was not a *Chela* and never appeared at our
gatherings, but she knew M.H. personally none
the less.

When I entered her drawing-room that afternoon I found Arkwright just saying good-bye
to a pretty but unrefined-looking woman who, I
thought, rather too markedly gave me the "glad
eye" as she passed out.

"Is it indiscreet to ask who that is?" I enquired when she had gone.

"Prostitute," returned Arkwright briefly.

I raised my eyebrows. "Reform?"

"Hardly."

"What's the idea then?"

"Oh—got talking one night, so thought I'd ask her to blow in sometime and see us."

"*Us?* . . . Then your wife doesn't object?"

"Object? Not *she*. They enjoy each other."

"Splendid!" I cried, "there are jolly few people like *you* two . . . M.H. know?"

"Yep."

"What does he say?"

"Approves, of course; ran up against her himself one day in this very room and talked a bit of mild philosophy to her."

"Wish I'd been there. How did she take it?"

"She was tickled to death."

"Didn't ask her to chuck her job?"

"You wouldn't expect him to act like a Salvation Army tambourine-clapper, would you?"

"Well, no . . ." I laughed.

"Besides, it wouldn't be the least good in this case."

"I daresay not—But I still don't quite get the idea."

"See here, Broadbent," he began, fiddling with one of my coat-buttons, "why d'you suppose one of the great Indian Mahatmas lets a lot of primitive Thibetan peasants hang around

his house just to get perhaps nothing more than
a smile ? "

" But does he ? " I was doubtful.

" Yes, he does . . . Well, God knows I'm no
Master, nor anywhere near being one, but don't
you think even you and I, just because we're
linked up with *our* Master and with all he stands
for, must give out something that's going to
help people like that prostitute, even if they
don't know it ? "

" You mean that just being within one's
aura must have an effect ? "

" Why, of course . . . *She* thinks she only
comes here for sympathy, and all that—and she
gets it ; but she gets something else she doesn't
know of, and which may not show up in this
incarnation at all. We're influencing her ego
or her soul, whichever you like to call it,
even if we don't talk one word of our philosophy."

" Then you don't believe in this occultist-talk
about contamination and the dangers of keeping
bad company ? " I teased him.

" Gee, it makes me tired ! " he exploded,
nearly pulling off my button. " Are you never
going to help some poor devil in a slum, because
you may get a bit of dirt on your pants by sitting

on his floor? Gosh, I'd go to bed with that
woman if I thought any good'd come of it!"

I had to laugh at his splendid downrightness.
"What would M.H. say to that?" I queried.

"Never asked him, but I can guess. I know
he often wants us to do strange sort of things
which would seem to be sheer waste of time,
and then when we've done them, he tells us the
reason . . . You know Herbert?"

"The musician-*chela*?"

Arkwright nodded. "When Herbert went
to Chicago for a month, M.H. specified the
very boarding-house he was to stay at—a poor
kind of place, and Herbert's a rich man—and
he was told to play to a lot of unmusical people
nearly every evening, or whenever they asked
him, even though they couldn't really understand the sort of music he played. There were
old ginks in that boarding-house with auras as
foul as dung-heaps. What price contamination
there?"

"Yes, but could he do any good?" I questioned.

"My friend," said a gentle and familiar voice
behind me, "the vibrations of good music are
beneficial at all times, but when set in motion
by one who is consciously doing the Master's
work, they are doubly so."

I turned round to encounter M.H.'s smile, and wondered how long he had been in the room. Then Wilson, another *Chela*, arrived.

"Excuse me," he groaned, sinking into the first handy chair, "but I'm drained out."

"What's the trouble?" asked M.H. cheerfully.

"My wife—hysterics—for two hours. This is the third attack in two days I've had to cope with."

M.H. put his hand on Wilson's for a moment, and his voice was full of tenderness and sympathy as he said: "My son, a very trying wife affords a golden opportunity for progress to the soul advanced enough to profit by it. You *are* advanced enough, so take comfort."

Wilson looked at him gratefully.

"You are learning your lesson, and when it has been learnt to the full, there will be no more hysterics."

"Devilish sorry for you, old man," murmured Arkwright, "had a bit of a bad time myself with Ella over this new kid of ours: she wanted a boy, and it's a girl. Queer how some women get disgruntled over a thing like that."

"The sexual instinct in an insidious form," said M.H.

"Is that so?" Arkwright asked.

M.H. nodded. "But you needn't tell your wife," he smiled, "just *yet*."

"And that reminds me, what's got the girl?" exclaimed Arkwright, suddenly jumping up and going out of the room; we heard him calling: "Honey!" in the passage.

"It's all very well," Wilson remarked, "but there are a great many fathers who are every bit as keen on having sons as Ella Arwright seems to be."

"That's often vanity," said M.H. "When a man is afraid his family will die out, that means he's proud of it. How much better to be an old soul in a young family than a young soul in an old family!"

Arkwright came back into the room bringing his wife with him. She carried a baby in her arms.

"*So* sorry . . ." she lamented without a trace of affectation, "you *will* forgive me—And I can't even shake hands. Here's the baby . . ." she added, showing it to M.H. We others politely crowded round to look. "But you needn't admire it and act silly," she assured us, "I just want *his* blessing on it, though it *is* a girl!"

M.H. laughed quietly and stroked the childs'

forehead with the tips of his fingers. "And you have it . . ." he assured her in return.

"Teach me not to mind its being a girl . . ." she coaxed with vivacious *naiveté*, heeding my presence as little as if we had known each other since childhood instead of having only met at that moment.

"We Gurus are not omnipotent," he reminded her, "and you are asking much. But perhaps I can give you an idea that may help you to teach yourself. It is not a new idea but a very ancient one. Let us leave your own case aside for a moment. We will suppose some other woman has a baby ; she loves that baby and imagines she loves it simply because it is a baby. It grows into a child, and although it is no longer a baby she loves it nevertheless and imagines she is loving it for its childishness. It then becomes a youth, and although it's no longer a baby or even a child she still loves it and imagines she is loving it because of its youthfulness. Finally it becomes a man and she has probably become an old woman, but although ever so many years have passed since it was a baby her love is as great as ever. And then at last she realises that the reason for her love couldn't have been its babyhood or childhood or youth at all: every one of these changing states has disappeared. Then what is the secret of her love? She loves it for itself—the soul which has no sex, and of which sex is merely a changing manifestation." He paused and looked at her kindly. "And now do you see what I mean?"

She put her head against Arkwright's shoulder and answered: "Yes, I think perhaps just a little . . . but please what have I got to do about it?"

We all laughed at the quaintness of her. "You have to exercise the will to love—or, better said, the imagination to love," was the Master's reply.

"The trouble with you, Honey," said Arkwright caressing her, "is that you're a bit too advanced to act like the ordinary mother and slobber over your baby like a cow over its calf, and you—"

"What's that you're saying, Honey?" she interrupted.

"I was saying," (he winked at us) "that you just fall between two stools. You're beyond the animal-instinct stage, which makes mothers and animals proud to bursting when they've produced a kid, and—er—well, you haven't quite reached the other stage yet that M.H. talked about."

" I expect you'd have felt just the same," Wilson put in sympathetically, " if it *had* been a boy."

" Why, surely ! " Arkwright exclaimed, " only she doesn't realise it."

" And I've forgotten about the tea ! " she exclaimed going off at a tangent; and with the baby still in her arms, hurried away.

*   *   *   *   *   *

Half an hour later I was sitting beside M.H. in his motor.

" I think that Arkwright girl's a real sport," I remarked, " Arkwright told me about their prostitute friend."

" Yes, Ella has a beautiful nature," he agreed cordially.

I was inquisitive enough to ask why she never came to the talks.

" She is not exactly an accepted *chela*," was the answer.

"I should have thought anyone as tolerant—" I began, then stopped when I saw his look of mild amusement.

" If all the *tolerant* people in America had to be accommodated with seats in my house. . . ."

I laughed.

"Still, there are other reasons," he conceded, "Arkwright is a poor man ; that girl fulfils the duties of wife, mother, nurse and servant. She is progressing quicker in that unassuming way than by the more spectacular method of joining the Order. Besides, Arkwright can pass on as much of the teaching as I feel justified in giving her at present."

"And yet she seems to regard you as her Master," I objected.

"You are mistaken. She doesn't know *consciously* what a Master means, as *you* understand the term, and she mustn't be told."

I looked at him in astonishment.

"There are scores of mystical and occult societies all over America," he explained, "societies run by Sufis, by Vendantins, by Theosophists, and many other heterodox persons. *She* looks upon me as the Head of some occult order, that's all—and having a nature rich in love and faith, she regards me in much the same light as a devout Roman Catholic regards her father-confessor. And by the way, those many heterodox orders are very useful to me—they ward off the curiosity-mongers. People who hear of us at all, say vaguely :

'Oh, yes, those theosophical people who've started a branch of their own. . . .'"

"But isn't it awkward," I asked, returning to the subject of the Arkwrights, "when the husband's a *chela* and the wife isn't?"

"Awkwardness may teach many things," was the reply, "*he* learns discretion and *she* learns to overcome curiosity."

And I wondered at that moment if M.H. did not think *I* was being unduly curious. . . .

Later on I discovered that he had not told me everything. The more I saw of Ella Arkwright herself, the more evident it became to me that she suffered from the defects which were the concomitants of her very engaging virtues. That effervescent naive candour of hers was coupled with an indiscretion which would have proved very inconvenient to a Master. To entrust her with some of the teachings M.H. imparted, would have been to incur the danger of their eventually getting into wrong hands.

CHAPTER X

"WILL you come in for our meal?" M.H. asked when we arrived at his door, " I shall be busy for about half an hour with my secretary, or rather my *chela* who acts as secretary, but after that I'm free for a while. You can always find a book to pass the time."

I was of course glad to do as he suggested.

M.H. had two *chelas* living in the house with him : a young Singhalese and the secretary-*chela* just mentioned, a man named Heddon. After the meal was over (I noticed M.H. hardly ate anything himself), and we were smoking excellent cigars, I asked, in the course of conversation, what his views were concerning the future of the Theosophical Society.

"That depends to a large extent on the behaviour of Theosophists," he answered with one of his graver smiles. "Though the Society does not exactly come under my surveillance, I am interested in its career, and it has already done and may continue to do very good work. Unfortunately I see in some of the Theosophists themselves faults both serious and trifling, but the trifling ones occasionally have as far-reaching adverse results as the serious ones."

"What sort of faults?" Heddon enquired. He appeared to know very little about the Society and its doings.

"Well—for instance, I think it's sad to see members of a Society which professes Brother-hood engaged in civil warfare with words—which is only one degree better than waging it with blows. From the very beginning the Society has at fairly close intervals been pre-occupied with quarrelling in one form or another, and what should best be ignored or tolerantly forgiven, becomes augmented into a scandal, so that members leave their Lodges in a body by way of protest, their chests expanded in an exhibition of what they take to be *righteous* indignation.

"The bellows of conviction," murmured the Singhalese drily.

M.H. nodded. "In an occult journal I've read acrimonious letters relating to the ordina-

tion of Bishops and whether it was justified or
not, and latterly there has arisen a movement
which, on the assumption that Madame Blavatsky said the last word on occult wisdom, condemns all newer teaching as a sign of disloyalty
to her memory."

" Why, I thought," was my comment, " that
even while she was still alive the Masters
pointed out that as yet they had only 'lifted a
corner of the veil,' and admitted that with all
her qualities she wasn't entirely reliable in some
respects."

" So they did," replied M.H.

" And what is the root-*cause* of all these—
shall we say blemishes on the Theosophical
escutcheon ?" in the calm soft voice of the
Singhalese. "Lack of control; control of temper,
control of emotion, and control of the tongue."

" And its effect," said M.H. taking him up,
" the alienation of those who might join the
Society and reap the benefits for which it was
founded."

" Deaf people cannot hear loud noises," remarked the Singhalese in his measured way,
" but they can often hear soft whispers."

M.H., seeing my puzzled expression, looked
at me with a twinkle, then at his *chela.* " You

musn't expect two poor matter-of-fact Occiden-
tals always to understand your profound similes
without elucidation," he teased him.

The Singhalese smiled in a manner that
endeared him to me at once—it was so utterly
devoid of superiority.   "Our Theosophical
friends are deaf," he explained, "because although they can hear the soft whispers from the
astral planes, they cannot hear the loud voice
of Reason telling them that intolerance can never
be compatible with the spirit of Brotherhood."

"I now understand," said I, bowing.

"And those minor faults you spoke of?"
Heddon asked M. H.

"They are trifles, I admit, and I hope and
think we Brothers are the last to be intolerant.
But—to show you what I mean—when I sometimes focus my consciousness on a theosophical
gathering, I see far too many peculiar, vague,
sloppy, absent-minded and unpractical dreamers
who perhaps ask : 'And what can *I* do for the
Masters . . .?' and who, when told, are unwilling to comply because the very thing the
Masters want them to do isn't spectacular enough
to appeal to them."   He smiled indulgently.   "I
remember not so very long ago trying again and
again to impress upon the consciousness of a

certain woman that she must cease to deny her husband his conjugal rights, and thus cease to act in the selfish manner she was then doing. But I could make no headway whatever, because she was so obsessed by high-falutin' ideas of so-called purity that she was deaf to the promptings of my still, small voice trying to speak to her ego. Neither Theosophy nor any other form of occultism," he continued after a pause, "should be used as a pretext for conjugal selfishness. It must never render women (*or* men) neglectful of their duties, nor render them vague and unpractical. After all, the practical lesson which Theosophy has to teach is that of Control. Selfishness in any form, lack of common-sense and all kindred weaknesses are symptoms of un-control. Whenever possible I like my *chelas* to teach Theosophists to be a credit to and an advertisment for their Society, not the reverse, as some of them are. Merely to believe in the doctrines of Karma and Reincarnation, for instance, may prove a consolation to them personally, but how will it benefit others who as yet do not believe in these doctrines? Besides, these two doctrines are not absolute essentials : they are but two of the many facets of the great Diamond of Truth."

M. H. rose from his chair and began pacing up and down.

"Even what is true, when over-emphasised, may assume the proportions of a dogma," I suggested.

"Certainly," he replied. "I find, for instance, that a lot of members of the Theosophical Society lay far too much stress on Karma, as *they* understand the word. In young and unevolved souls it is often productive of valetudinarianism. The would-be interesting man or woman—usually woman—says: 'I am ill—it is my Karma—I must bear it . . .' And she feels quite proud of the fact, or what she considers to be the fact. But if we probe into her subconsciousness we find it is not her 'Karma'—" he again smiled indulgently—"but her vanity which lies at the root of the trouble, and which prompts the desire to draw attention to herself. As you know, in this circle here we employ the word Karma in its more literal sense—as the Law of Cause and Effect in relation to *all* actions, and not merely to those of past incarnations. We say, for example, if a man gets drunk one night that the splitting headache with which he wakes up next morning is his Karma!"

We had to laugh at this.

"And why?" continued M.H., ignoring our amusement, "because it is the effect of a cause —in other words, that man is paying up, *not* for the sins of a previous incarnation but for those of a previous night. If Karma is merely understood in the restricted sense in which the more narrow-minded Theosophists understand it, those evils arise—valetudinarianism and others —which we try to avoid here. So you'll benefit them by teaching them that the results of Karma are nothing whatever to be proud of, and that the sooner they cease to give the doctrine such undue prominence, the better." He stopped to re-light his cigar. "Altogether I am sorry to see an attitude of dogmatism among Theosophical members—some of them go so far as to think that they *as* Theosphists have the exclusive right to attention from the Masters. They'd doubtless get a shock if you told them that there is many an atheist and even a harlot more receptive to the teachings of the Masters than they are. This dogmatic type of Theosophist is the exact opposite to the vague woolly-minded type—which at least usually has a good deal of love in its make-up—and is, spiritually speaking, worse off because imbued with a quite unconscious conventionalism.

The mental bodies of such people are hard and
unyielding; because they have embraced an
unconventional religion, they think themselves
correspondingly unconventional. But they're
mistaken : within the confines of their Theosophical outlook, they're nearly as narrow and
sectarian as the most bigoted of Christians."

"They should beware of Theosophical Pharisaism," the Singhalese observed, "for although
the Masters' love shines upon them as the great
orb of day, the windows of their minds and hearts
may be too small to give it entrance."

"Thank you, my son," said M. H. with quiet
humour.   Then, becoming more serious: "The
Theosophical Society stands at a very critical
moment of its career.   It may continue to grow
in membership, but unfortunately the size of a
Society is not necessarily what counts, but the
quality of it.   If the Society is to remain a great
force for good in the world, and I fervently hope
it will do so, then for one thing its members must
uproot cowardice.   There have been cowards
who have run away at the moment of danger,
and instead of giving a hand at the pumps, have
deserted the ship.   It doesn't matter whether the
danger has appeared in the form of a scandal,
having for its basis some kink in the nervous

system of one of its members, or whether dis-
sensions have arisen around opinions and pro-
nouncements about the World Teacher. If
Brotherhood means anything at all, it means
standing by one another not only in moments
of safety but also in danger. To my mind the
future of the Theosophical Society depends
before all else on the moral heroism of its
members."

CHAPTER XI

THE EPISODE IN THE CHURCHYARD

THE Sunday on which M.H. had promised to take us into the country turned out a gorgeous day. We were to start at 10 o'clock and he was to call for me at my club, and then pick up Viola Brind afterwards. Punctual to the minute he appeared at my door and we set out immediately; but instead of making direct for Viola's house, he turned off in another direction.

"Hullo," I said, "isn't Miss Brind coming after all, or have you forgotten about her?"

"She's coming all right," he answered with a mysterious smile, "but I've got to pick up somebody else first."

"Another of our circle?"

He nodded, but didn't give me any further information.

Only when we drew up in front of Clare's door did I get my answer.

"A pleasant little surprise for you," he said, " I 'phoned Clare Delafield to come with us."

We had a most exhilarating run. Viola sat in front with M.H., so I had Clare to myself in the back of the car. All the same he did not ignore us completely, but from time to time turned half round to us and either commented on the scenery or shouted the names of the villages through which we passed. We had been driving for about two hours and a half when we arrived at a picturesque little place where it was decided that we should get out and have lunch. We drew up in front of a small hotel, but as it was still early for the midday meal, M.H. suggested we should take a stroll and look round the village. There was an old church surrounded by a churchyard a few paces from the hotel, and towards this we wandered. As we entered the gate, a few lingerers from morning service were talking to one another prior to going home; but they soon dispersed, and the churchyard was left empty save for one young girl whom I noticed standing a little way off among the graves. We sauntered about, looking at the various monuments and their inscriptions, till finally we came quite close up to this girl. Then I saw that she was laying

flowers on a new grave.   She looked so sorrowful that I felt I would have given anything to
be able to comfort her.   But *what* could I say
that might have any effect?   Also, I was far too
diffident to talk to a stranger.   I was thinking
these thoughts when, chancing to look towards
M.H., who was a few feet in front, I noticed
that he was gazing intently at the girl.   The
next moment he went up to her and laid a hand
on her shoulder.

"My child," he said with a great depth of
tenderness, "don't grieve for your father like
this.   He's not down there in that grave, he's
standing beside you and telling you he has
never left you."

She evidently did not grasp his full meaning
for she clutched his hand and exclaimed : " You
knew my father ? "

"No, my child."

"Then—I—I don't understand—I've never
seen you before.   How—how could you know?"
She hastily withdrew her hand.

"Because I see his spirit here now and can
hear him saying : 'Tell her not to go under
like that, I'm her Dad—help her to understand
I've never left her.'"

She turned away and hung her head, as if

utterly at a loss what to think or say, but she did not weep.

M.H. put his arm round her shoulder and drew her towards him. "Come, my child," he said very gently, "I'm here to comfort you; won't you listen?"

She felt for his hand, clutched it once more and gave a little nod, but seemed unable to speak. I looked at Viola and Clare and saw their eyes were full of tears.

"Listen," the Master said in a low voice, "some of us can see those whom people wrongly call the dead, for there are no dead really. I know this may be hard to believe but it's true. Shall I tell you what your father is like to help you to understand?"

She did not answer but made an almost imperceptible gesture of assent.

"He is still young, only about thirty-eight— clean-shaven, tall, and has such a . . ."

She suddenly began to sob.

"There, there, my child," he soothed her, "don't do that. I understand—but don't cry." He stroked her hand and waited for a few moments. "Do you know what I was just going to say?" he asked encouragingly. "It was that your father would be perfectly happy where he is if what *you* are feeling didn't hurt him so much.   Won't you try not to be unhappy for *his* sake ? "

" It's—so hard . . ." she sobbed.

" I know, my dear, I know—but think what it means to him to see you so miserable, and when he tries to comfort you to find that you can't hear his voice !   Wouldn't *you* feel badly if that happened to you ? "

She nodded again.

"You were more pals than father and daughter. Isn't that so ? "   He spoke now in a more conversational voice that gave the impression that he wanted to divert her attention.   " But if it weren't possible for some of us to *see* those who have left their bodies how could I know all this ?   It *wouldn't* be possible, would it ?   So you see although we *think* our loved ones die and go far away, or fade out of existence altogether they don't really ; they're with us all the time, only we're not all able to perceive them and hear what they say.

She ceased to sob.

" You are a lovely man," she said with an inflection which caused Clare to put her handkerchief to her eyes.

M. H. smiled.   "That's better," he said cheerfully. "And now, my child, your father wants me to give you a message. Oh—and your mother's here too. You hardly remember her, do you? She died when you were so young."

The girl looked almost happy in her amazement.

"Well, now, I'll repeat word for word what I hear your father say: 'Tell—my—little—one —I—am—not—down—*there*—but—am—right —here—on—the—spot—with—Mamma—Tell —her—I—don't—want—her—come—to—this —place—any—more—it—makes—her—feel— badly—because—she—suffers—Ask—her—to pay—attention—to—what—Mrs.—Hodge— says—she—can—help—her—also—I—should —be—very—grateful—if—the—small—fair— young—lady—with—you—will—extend—her —friendship—to—my—little—one—I—have —gotten—her—thoughts—and—know—she— can—see—us—Mamma—and—I—send— more—love—than—we—can—put—into— words—and—implore—our—little—one—for— the—love—of—Mike—not—to—grieve—And —now—I—thank—you—sir—for—the— service—you—have—rendered—us—we—are —more—than—indebted—to—you—Tell—the —little—one—this—is—a—damn—fine—place

—but—we—are—always— around — *always*—
you—understand — though — I — guess — it—
sounds—a—bit—queer—to—her — but — your
—friend—will—make—her — understand—one
—of—these—days—Please—persuade — her—
to—go—back — home — now — and — once—
more—thank—you.' That's the message, my
child, so you see everything's not so dreadful
after all, is it? And my friend here will give
you more messages some time; she'll arrange
for you to come and see her in Boston. You
often run over to Boston, don't you?"

The girl smiled and said she did, and Viola
who had moved to her side, asked her name
and address and gave her own.

"So now," said M. H., patting her shoulder,
"I would get along home to your sister, if I
were you. And just think of your father as
having gone on a splendid holiday—for that's
all it really is. And don't forget, you *will*
hear from him again, we'll see to that all right.
Good-bye, my child," he held out his hand,
"God bless you."

She took his hand and lifted it to her lips.
"God bless *you*," she said, "I—I can't tell
you all you've done for me. I shall never
forget this to—to the end of my life."

She turned to Viola. "And thank *you*," she extended her hand, but instead of taking it, Viola put her arms round her and kissed her.

"And will you come and see me too?" Clare said huskily.

"Surely I will," she answered with emotion.

We watched her as she made her way out of the churchyard. I had such a pronounced lump in my throat that I could not have spoken without disgracing myself. It was, I believe, just because M.H. realised what we were all feeling, that in his quite normal and cheerful voice he said: "It's good to know that three people are the happier as the result of this excursion. But," glancing at his watch, "it's after one o'clock; we'd better be moving lunch-wards."

Clare's eyes were still rather red when we sat down to luncheon.

"Upset you a bit, eh?" said M.H. with one of his most affectionately encouraging smiles. "Let's think of something else, then."

She gave him a look of gratitude. "Feeling sorry for people is painful."

"I confess I find it painful too," I said, "what about you, Miss Brind?"

"I think it's horribly painful."

"Compassion takes people in various ways,"
M.H. mused, "it's largely a matter of temperament—until, of course, one gets beyond the
dictates of temperament.

"You mean when one's reached Bliss-consciousness?" I said.

He nodded. "Compassion acts as a means
of making us feel love for the time being.
That's why it *can* be a very pleasant sensation.
But it becomes unpleasant if instead of identi-
fying our minds with our love-sensation, we
get swept up in the sufferings of the person
towards whom we are feeling compassionate."

"But isn't it very difficult not to get swept
up?" Clare asked.

"That depends on the stage of our evolution.
In any case it's a pity to get bowled over, as
it hinders our capacity to help. A doctor
wouldn't be much good if he fainted or wept
at the sight of an accident, would he?"

"That's true enough," I agreed.

"It sounds a hard thing to say," M.H.
continued, "but a certain type of compassion
contains an element of selfishness and cowardice.
How is it, for instance, that when you hear
of a terrible railway accident in India or somewhere very far away, you're hardly even in-

terested, but when you hear of a similar accident in Boston you're dreadfully upset, and can't get the thing out of your heads for days? It's because you unconsciously think you might have been in that accident—or might have lost a friend in it."

"What you say there *has* always struck me as curious," Viola remarked, "but I never thought of that explanation."

"I think it's the true one all the same. Or put it another way," the Master elaborated, "when a child breaks one of its toys and sets up ear-splitting cries, you don't immediately feel inclined to start crying too. You smile and pet the child and hug it a little, and there the matter ends. Because you as a grown-up person know perfectly well that the breaking of a toy couldn't upset *you* like that—which simply means that you're not afraid of such a thing happening to yourselves."

"That's a very ingenious argument," I exclaimed, "but distinctly unflattering to one's vanity."

M.H. laughed. "You shouldn't have any," he teased me.

"Ah, if one were rid of *that*——" I returned.

"Still," he continued, "the real compassion

which contains no element of selfishness or cowardice is a beautiful and quite painless emotion; it is even a joyful emotion, because it's the outcome of pure love, and pure love is always joyful."

"Yet Christ is said to have wept," I observed.

"You mustn't believe everything you read in the Bible, you know, or you'll find yourself in difficulties. That story about Jesus weeping when He hears that Lazarus is dead, doesn't bear looking into. Why should He weep if He knew it was possible to bring the man back to life again, or if He realised he wasn't dead—put which interpretation you like upon it!"

"Mightn't He have wept out of pity for the others—I mean Mary and Martha?" I hazarded.

M.H. shook his head. "It won't work, my friend; *such* a manifestation of compassion would have been weakness. What would you think of a doctor who, although he realised perfectly that his patient could be saved, nevertheless burst into tears when told by the relatives that that patient was ill? Surely that would be the best way to frighten them out of their lives."

We all had to laugh at this.

"I *must* say to waste time in weeping instead

of immediately getting to work to remove the *cause* of such weeping would be very queer behaviour—and certainly not the behaviour of an Adept.   No, I think we'll have to fall back on the 'tears of joy' theory, as Shri Parananda does in his Eastern exposition of the Gospels : two excellent books, by the way, which I strongly advise you to read."

The conversation was interrupted by the negro waiter who wanted to hand the next course, but M.H. had been so busy talking that he had forgotten to eat.   So he hastily finished what was on his plate.

"Last time I was here," he said, affably addressing the waiter, "we had the best waffles I've ever tasted for a long time."

The waiter beamed, showing a row of ivory white teeth.   " Guess you won't be disappointed with to-day's lot either," he said.

"Well, I hope not.   By the way, I notice none of you are very upset at the tears of the little boy at the next table," he added quizzically to us.

We glanced in the direction where a pater-familias in company with his wife and the little boy, was urging the latter to finish up a far too large helping of meat and potatoes.

"And *I* notice you don't go and play the good Samaritan this time," I teased back.

" Wouldn't do," he laughed, " they'd only resent it.   You can't make parents understand," he went on in an undertone, "that it's a great mistake to make children eat when they've no appetite or have eaten enough.   Nature's got to get rid of all that excess of food somehow and sometime.   However that's no reason why *we* shouldn't have some more waffles.   Samuel!" he called.

The waiter appeared.

"More waffles, please."

It was dark before we reached Boston again where I was to complete the day by dining with Clare.

"See you Wednesday," said M.H. as he deposited us in front of her house.

CHAPTER XII

QUESTIONS ON MARRIAGE

THERE were two evenings a month on which instead of listening to a set discourse from M.H., the *chelas* were encouraged to ask questions on any subject that occurred to them. He made a rule, however, that when once a subject was introduced all questions must bear relation to it —this policy being adopted, as he had once explained, in order to ensure consecutiveness of thought.

One of the *chelas*, a Frenchman, who, I was told, had acquired extraordinary physical control —he could hold his breath for a prodigious length of time, stop his heart, and perform other remarkable Yogic feats—put the question, with a strong foreign accent : " Say, Master, do you considair marriage compateeble with spiritual advancement ? "

"That's a very foolish question from *you*," M.H. replied, the stern inflection of his voice immediately quelling a ripple of subdued amusement. "Have you been here all these years to such poor purpose that you don't know the answer without asking *me*?"

"Then why do the Indian books on Yoga tell that it is *not*?" the Frenchman persisted, though he looked uncomfortable after the rebuke.

"I should have thought you might have known that too," M.H. answered regretfully. "How often must I hammer it into your consciousness that you are too lop-sided, and that one day you will have to go back and learn all that you have missed. Answer him!" he ordered the Singhalese who was sitting in the front row.

"The Indian books you speak of," replied the *chela* in his usual dispassionate manner, "were written *by* Yogis for *aspiring* Yogis. Their teachings are only suitable to European conditions when subjected to a process of selection and adaptation. That is what the Gurus are for. As to marriage, it brings bondage to fools and spiritual progress to wise men; it is a playground with many dangers for children, and a school for the enlightened. It is that fertile ground on which may be grown the beautiful flowers of a hundred virtues, or the noisome weeds of a hundred vices."

" Do you consider," one of the woman-*chelas* asked M.H., " that people are beginning to understand the spiritual value of marriage ? "

" In Europe and America," every trace of sternness had disappeared from his voice, "alas, very few people indeed understand its true value. And at present the whole attitude towards matrimony is a disastrous one, which, instead of leading to contentment and spiritual progress, leads to the divorce-court. So long as jealousy is regarded as a reputable passion, and romantic infatuation is considered the chief *raison d'être* for entering wedlock, how can we expect it to be otherwise?" He paused, waiting for a further question.

" Do you mean to say," demanded a novelist sitting beside me, " that romantic love is *never* a secure foundation for marriage?"

" Wise men," M. H. replied, "are chary of bringing the word *never* into any argument. Romantic infatuation is very *seldom* a secure foundation for marriage—except in novels," he added, twinkling.

There was a laugh in which the novelist joined.

"And yet in countries where the laws are easy," M. H. resumed, "when people who have married for pleasure on the strength of an infatuation, find themselves unsuited to one another, instead of trying to learn the lesson their egos (higher selves) wish them to learn, they shirk it and, like cowards, run away—to the divorce courts.   Because it is too much trouble to adapt themselves, and conquer the dislike and irritation they feel towards each other once the glamour has worn off, they seek the easiest way out of the dilemma.   Rather than obey the dictates of the higher self, they listen to the voice of the lower self which says : 'You *thought* you loved this man or woman—you've been cheated—so make an end of it and separate for ever.'"

"But how are you going to prevent people marrying because they're in love ?" I asked.

"By gradually setting before them a higher ideal.   It will take a long time, but what of that? Teach them to marry neither for passion, pleasure, nor, as goes without saying, for material advantage."

"What do *you* mean by passion ?" somebody inquired, "the purely physical ?"

"You do well to ask that question," he

answered, "because the word is often employed in a far too arbitrary sense. Will anybody oblige?"

"I should say there are three forms of passion," I hazarded, "one, the purely physical; one, though rarer, the purely sentimental; and one, the sentimental-physical."

M. H. nodded.

"And it strikes me," said a very American voice, "that what our friend calls the sentimental and the sentimental-physical give the knock-out blow to a man's judgment a daft sight sooner than any sheer unvarnished lust I was ever ashamed of in the days of my youth!"

M. H. broke into a hearty laugh. "We are getting along," he observed, "any more confessions forthcoming?"

"Every romantic affair *I've* ever had," said another man, "has ended in smoke, so I wouldn't give a damn for one of them. But I can imagine having a very deep and lasting friendship for several women, with any one of whom one could pass a very pleasant night—and it's one of those women I'd marry if I wanted to marry at all."

"Or if *I* wanted you to marry," M. H. corrected, "which is more important."

" Or *you*—a sure thing ! "

" So you see, though our friend has expressed it in a manner perhaps a little shocking to a Victorian old maid, he has implied that companionship marriage is the only marriage likely to endure."

" That's all very well," said Viola, " but if you tell people to marry simply for friendship, they think you mean a Platonic marriage."

" For what have you a tongue, my child, but to tell people what you *do* mean ? "

" Then you don't approve of Platonic marriages ? " I inferred.

"If two people who are mentally sympathetic but physically antipathetic wish to marry, that hardly concerns a Guru in his—shall I say official capacity . . . But except in very rare instances, I do not advise enforced Platonicism. These Platonic marriages which occur nowadays between people belonging to various mystical and occult societies, are symptomatic of a false conception of so-called purity.   These good people are trying to progress too fast ; and because they are attempting to run with their spiritual feet before they can walk, they are engendering nervous complaints and other evils.   The women become hysterical and often suffer from uterine troubles which cloud their judgment and hinder their general activities; and the men suffer from irritability, neurasthenia, and such complaints as occur when there is no Guru handy to teach them how to avoid these results. They say to themselves: 'We are making ourselves purer vehicles for the Masters to work through . . .' and the books that they read, full of beautiful sentiments, uphold them in their belief. Some of these well-meaning but misguided people have been monks, nuns or ascetics of a sort in their last lives. Yet why do you suppose in this life they have been born into the noise and turmoil of a European or American civilisation? It is in order to learn a different lesson—to learn the particular lesson this civilisation—such as it is—has to teach. But if they merely try to repeat their last lesson, so to say, in a different environment, they are wasting their incarnation. I will tell you a little piece of occult news.—Not so long ago a great Yogi lived in India; so much revered was he, that when he was expected in the big towns, the buildings were decorated with flags and the streets with festoons. That-Yogi died, and is now reincarnated as *a little girl* in England. What a 'come-down,' the unenlightened will say! But no. The ego of that Yogi has still something to learn, and he can only learn it in a female body and in the western world, even though he is nearing Masterhood. And what's more, if this soul carries out the programme the Gurus have planned, that erstwhile Yogi may marry and have children.

"And so what I'd impress upon you is to help people to learn the lesson their particular environment has to teach. If they are married, they should fulfil all the obligations of marriage, so that they may come to cultivate those virtues which marriage can educe. It is you who must begin to teach mankind the Super-morals of marriage."

He paused, and a rather shy voice from a pupil who had only recently entered our order asked: "And please, what are the super-morals of marriage?"

"Tell him," said M. H. kindly to the Singhalese.

"Conjugal super-morality is conjugal un-selfishness pursued to its logical conclusion," came the answer.

"Give him a practical example," said M.H.

"If a woman desires a child and her husband is impotent or sterile, he should permit her to have a child by another man, if she so wishes."

"Good!" said M.H., and the new *chela's* face was a study.

"But," objected the Frenchman, "if that woman is married with a 'usband 'oo is sterile, it is 'er Karma!"

"Someone answer him!" M.H. ordered sharply.

The Singhalese again volunteered: "If a woman is drowning in a river, and two men are standing on the bank, one who can swim and one who can*not*, shall the man who cannot swim pinion the other man and say: 'Leave her to drown, it is her bad Karma?'"

"Precisely," said M.H., "how can *he* know that it's not her bad Karma merely to get a fright or a ducking or to spoil her newest dress?"

All the women laughed.

"Besides," he continued, "what about the good Karma the other man would make by rescuing her? No—let us teach husbands and wives to leave the workings of Karma to the Lords of Karma. The duty of all super-moralists is to act in accordance with the highest principles of unselfishness, and leave the consequences in Higher Hands. It is these principles, and these only, which can save the marriage-state from the chaotic condition into which it has fallen.

Marriage as it is at present exacts too much from human nature on the one hand, and too little on the other. In countries like Italy and Spain it allows a man to behave like a despot, and expects a woman to behave like a saint. This despotism is hidden under a fig-leaf on which are the words *preserving my honour*, but it is despotism all the same, and the matrix of brutality, cruelty, and even murder. *Preserving my honour* means in plainer words *preserving my vanity and my selfishness*—hence all the tragedies that ensue."

"Then do you consider conjugal fidelity so unimportant," the new *chela* asked, "that its breach ought not to be punished?"

"Fidelity, my son," was the gentle rejoinder, "is a virtue to be always *admired* but never exacted."

"But—" somebody was about to interrupt.

"One moment, my son, I've not finished. There is a form of fidelity which is far more important than sexual fidelity: that is the fidelity of mind and soul. To violate this involves much more serious consequences, because physical links are broken with the death of the body, whereas mental and spiritual links persist into future lives."

" I gather," said a man named Galais, the oldest of the *chelas* in point of years, " that you think the sexual fidelity which ordinary marriage teaches is not of great value, because it is largely the result of fear—I mean of a scandal or a divorce. What sort of lesson would that type of marriage teach in which fidelity was never *exacted*?"

" Many lessons, my son, but I will only mention one. It's easy enough to be gentle, kind and affectionate to our wives as long as we're in love with them, but it's not so easy when we're in love with somebody else. The man who, although he may be in love with another woman, can still be just the same kind, affectionate husband to his wife, has learnt to behave in accordance with that higher fidelity which is one of the lessons Free Marriage has to teach."

After that we broke up for the evening, but as I walked home with one of the *chelas* I asked : " Why was M.H. so down on the Frenchman?"

" Because although he's a damn fine nature he just won't absorb the philosophical side of the teaching. And he's got rather a thick hide too—gentle handling makes as little impression on it as a straw on a donkey's back."

I laughed.

"But don't get home with the idea," he continued, "that Master don't love him as much as any of us."

"How long has he been in the States?" I asked.

"About fifteen years."

"Then why hasn't he learnt better English?"

"You can search me—for the same reason he hasn't learnt philosophy, I guess!"

CHAPTER XIII

MYSTIFICATION

ALTHOUGH I saw the Master at the Friday evening lecture I had no private conversation with him. We merely exchanged a few words in the presence of the others ; he was going away the following morning and would be absent until Wednesday ; but in the interim he hinted that it would please him if I saw a little more of Viola Brind.

Was this hint intended to imply that hitherto I had not cultivated her to the extent he could have wished—or what ? I was becoming more and more mystified. Why always Viola Brind ? I even grew conscious of a little imp of the perverse which seemed to whisper : " You don't honestly like that girl, although you think you do. She's not the type that really appeals to you, so why not be quite frank about it ? If you hadn't been told to cultivate her you'd never have done so of your own accord, and you know it!" And I confess that much as I disliked this idea, contrary as it was to my Master's wishes, I could not help feeling at times that it was true, though at other times I shook it off and told myself it was absurd and nothing but imagination. *Of course* I liked the girl—why shouldn't I? There was nothing in her *to* dislike. Hadn't I been aware that we'd got on splendidly the last time we dined together—then why all of a sudden these misgivings? To hell with them—was I going to let such absurdities stand in the way of my Master's wishes? Surely he wasn't asking much of me—just to become friends with a clever and unusually gifted girl—if I couldn't accomplish *that*, I must indeed be a poor fool!

In any case, misgivings or not—I asked Viola to dine with me the very next day and she accepted. Nevertheless when she came I was, to my regret, aware of a slight feeling of hostility towards her. I could not pretend to account for it, but there it was. Just at that moment that second and lower self had evidently got the upper hand. And this was all the more strange, because by nature I am an expansive and affectionate person who seldom feels antagonistic to anybody. In fact my large heart has proved an inconvenience rather than otherwise—for when I meet people who appeal to me, I am apt to indulge in rather more demonstrativeness than is usually considered the correct thing.

Of course I quite made up my mind that I would on no account let Viola notice any change in my attitude towards her, but I did not altogether succeed, for we had been seated only a few minutes when she said reflectively: "Somehow you're not quite yourself to-night."

I was taken aback for a moment. "Do you know," I rejoined, "that phrase can be more literally true than is generally supposed. I don't altogether *feel* myself. Still, I hoped you wouldn't notice it. . . ."

"Why? Does it matter—my noticing it?"

I tried to laugh it off. "Oh, it's not of great importance, but, to tell the truth, I'm a little ashamed of it—it makes me feel awkward."

"I shouldn't worry about it."

"Do you know what it's like not to feel quite yourself?"

"Don't I just!"

I immediately became interested. "Tell me —you've got psychic powers—have you any idea why, without apparent rhyme or reason, one gets—it's a bit difficult to put into words—well,

the feeling that one part of oneself is suddenly
trying to prevent another part from doing a
particular thing—say something quite easy—
something one really wants to do?"

"It's hard to tell unless one knows the *sort*
of thing."

"Yes, I suppose it is," I conceded, not wishing
to commit myself any further."

"Can't you give me an instance?" she asked.

"It's not very easy——"

"You see, it might be something trivial—
something that any psycho-analyst could explain
—but it might also be something much more
formidable : I mean the 'Blacks.'"

"What do you mean by the 'Blacks'?"

"Don't you know?"—surprised—"the so-
called Brothers of the Left Hand Path.   The
ones who work against the Divine Will instead
of with It."

"Oh, *those* . . . Of course I know who *they*
are, but I didn't recognise them under that
name."   Then suddenly I had an impulse to
tell her the truth, but was checked by the
waitress handing the next course.

"Look here," I said, when she was out of
earshot, "we *are* excellent friends, aren't we?"

"I'm sure I *hope* so," she smiled.

"Then if I ask you something rather peculiar
—you'll understand?"

"Why, of course."

"Do you think the Blacks, as you call them,
might have reasons for wanting to smash up
our friendship?" I said slowly.

"It's quite possible—one can never tell what
they're up to. But why do you ask?"

"Because something has happened."

"Really—in what way?"

"I hardly like to tell you—but I'm going to
all the same." I hesitated for a moment, trying
to find words that would not seem too crude.
"I have a feeling," I said at last, "as if something were trying to stop me liking you—quite
so much."

She gave a curious little laugh. "That's
very peculiar," she said, "*I* have had the same
feeling too."

"You *mean* that?"

"I *mean* it—the Blacks are obviously trying
to get at both of us."

"But for heaven's sake why?" I exclaimed,
"what's the object of it?"

"Ah, goodness only knows! But I can tell
you this much: there's probably something
deeper in the whole matter than *we* know of.

When Master particularly wishes a thing, it's worth *their* while to try and stop it."

" You think it's as important as all that? "

" I suppose it *must* be."

We were again interrupted by the waitress.

" I'm not usually an inquisitive person," I said when the latter had withdrawn, " but upon my soul, I wish I knew what it all meant. Master gave me a hint on Friday to try and see more of you."

" He said pretty much the same to *me*.

I was more and more mystified.

" Do you know if he often does this sort of thing—I mean, is he often so keen that two people should—well—be special friends? "

" I've never *heard* so before, but then one doesn't hear everything," she paused for a moment. " *I'm* up against another mystery— talking of mysteries."

I looked at her questioningly.

" Master says one of these days he may be putting me a test I shan't altogether like."

" What sort of a test? " I asked, intensely interested.

" That's just what I don't know. He dropped the hint so that I should be prepared. All he said was that it'll be something in the nature of a sacrifice."

"Good Lord!" I exclaimed.

"Why do you look so surprised?"

"Because—— but let's go into the other room. It's usually empty and we can talk better there over our coffee."

"You were going to tell me something," she said when the coffee and smokes had been brought, and she had lit a cigarette.

"Do you happen to know why I came over here?" I asked.

"To be near Master, I suppose."

"That's one reason, but there's another. *He told me he had something in view which would mean making a sacrifice on my part.* Don't you think it's rather peculiar that he should say exactly the same thing to both of us?"

She gave a shrug. "Everybody who's with M.H. has to make sacrifices sooner or later: I don't think it necessarily has to do with you and me together."

"No, I quite admit I don't see how it *can*. First of all I can't imagine that anything in the way of work we had to do in conjunction could mean such a great sacrifice, secondly—— I've forgotten what I wanted to say, now!"

She laughed, then after a while mused : " Of course there *might* be some work he wanted us to do together which was something unpleasant and meant a good deal of self-sacrifice for both of us ; but I really can't imagine what sort of work it could be."

" And that might also be the reason why the Blacks are trying to get at us," I suggested.

" Quite possible."

I was silent for a few moments, trying to rack my brains for other solutions, but arrived at none.   Suddenly I said : " You're clairvoyant, can't you see into the future a bit ? "

She shook her head.   " I can never see anything to do with myself—clairvoyants never can, at my stage.   Besides——"

" Besides what ? "

" If M.H. intended us to know *now*, he'd have told us."

I felt I had been disloyal to my Master, and censured myself.   " You're quite right," I said, " we'd better give up all this speculating and wait and see what happens.   In the meantime we've got to prevent these Blacks from doing any damage.   This talk has done me good. When you first came this evening I felt awk-

ward, and I'll admit it—a bit hostile—but now
I'm all right again."

"Well, that's something to the good, at
any rate."

After that we talked on other subjects. We
also arranged to meet for tea on the Monday.
And as that same evening we were to dine
with Clare and her mother, and afterwards
go to a theatre, we both felt the Master would
not consider that his wishes had been dis-
regarded.

As for Clare and myself, we contrived to
see each other nearly every day, and most
of our interviews were undisturbed by the
presence of a third. Clare had her own little
studio, as she called it, and her very accom-
modating mother showed no surprise that we
should spend so much time in each other's
company. There was no deception about the
matter ; Mrs. Delafield knew that our feelings
for each other were of the nature of romance—
Clare had told her so—and she had accepted
the situation on the assumption that her
daughter was old enough to think and act for
herself. That in so doing she not only called
forth my admiration but also my gratitude, goes
without saying.

I was now passionately in love with Clare, and
I knew that my love was reciprocated. It is
said that a man of my age is apt to get the
"divine disease" very badly, and I felt this to
be true. Moreover it seemed to me this would
be my last romance—the last flicker of the
romantic fire before I reached that unconditional
Love-Consciousness which M.H. had promised
me *if*—if what ? For that was the mystery I
still came no nearer to solving. Rather had it
seemed to deepen after my conversation with
Viola. In any case—should I be able to fulfil
his conditions ? I did not see how it were
possible ever to fall in love again. As M.H.
had said " I should lose my heart permanently."
But to bring logic to bear on that metaphor, a
thing once lost forever cannot be lost a second
time ! Still, I might of course be wrong. When
this *permanent* Love-Consciousness did arrive,
so to say, it might be so different from what I
expected that many a possibility could arise
which I had not foreseen. There also came the
startling thought : suppose the sacrifice I was
called upon to make should be so great that I
could not face it ? It was unlikely ; but one can
never be absolutely certain of anything—except
the Absolute Itself . . . Still—I banished that

doubt almost as soon as it entered my head; I
utterly refused to entertain it. Had I not once
or twice tasted Unconditional Love-and-Bliss-
Consciousness, and ever since then known it to
be "the pearl of great price" for which one
would sell everything else—yes, even the prospect of *future* romances ?

Whether it was in answer to my speculations
that M. H. treated the whole subject of Love in
his discourses of the two following Wednesdays,
I cannot say. I was at this period never able
to guage to what extent he was conscious of my
unspoken thoughts and feelings. All the same
he did choose that subject, and as nothing
momentous happened to me in the intervening
week I am placing these two discourses in
successive chapters.

CHAPTER XIV

THE lecture that Wednesday evening was on "Maya and its relation to love;" but as much of it was of too intimate a nature to be suitable for publication, I can only give such portions as I consider advisable.

M.H. pointed out to begin with that much of what is termed Love is purely Maya—that is to say, Illusion. And yet Illusion is not an adequate translation of Maya, because this word does not mean non-existent or illusory like the objects in a dream, but a condition in which things appear to be as they are *not*, or in which we see things as they are *not*. Thus, much of what is taken for love is Maya, because it is fraught with illusions and engenders illusions in ourselves. "The unenlightened and the sentimental," he explained, "think love will last for ever, but it doesn't—and that is Maya; they think their loved ones are other than they prove to be—and that is Maya." And he went on to show us that a comprehension of this idea is very important, as one of the greatest aids to spiritual progress consists in the attempt to free ourselves from the thraldom of Maya.

"When we can see all things as they *are*, instead of as we desire them to be, then we shall have no more disappointments and few more sorrows.

"We find much of this thraldom of Maya in relation to marriage. The man who thinks he wants to live with a woman for a life-time and finds he doesn't want to live with her for a month is under the thraldom of Maya. The man who thinks a woman will be faithful to him till death, and finds she commits adultery with the first handsome soldier, is under the thraldom of Maya. And so on and so forth. We must endeavour to free ourselves from this thraldom, otherwise we shall never gain wisdom or come to know peace."

He furthermore maintained that we see much of this Maya-element in the prevalent attitude towards sexuality. To give an example: " The man who shoots or divorces his wife because she has had sexual intercourse with another man

shows at once that he attaches a prodigious importance to sexual intercourse itself; on the
other hand, the man who forgives his wife, or,
better still, does not even feel there is anything
to forgive, attaches little importance to sexual
intercourse itself, and therefore proves himself
to be not only a more evolved and enlightened
soul but a more chaste one as well.   Such a
man no longer sees either sexuality or marriage
through the veils of Maya."

M. H. next spoke of the prevalent misconcep-
tions regarding chastity, purity, and complete
abstinence.   "The chaste man," he explained,
"is not to our way of thinking here, the man
who practises complete sexual continence, but,
as I just implied, the man who sees sexuality
in its true light.   As nobody should be called a
gourmand who enjoys his dinner when hungry,
yet otherwise attaches little importance to eating, so nobody should be called unchaste who
enjoys the sexual act when the body demands it,
but otherwise is not preoccupied with sexuality
itself.   With regard to purity—what *we* mean
by the word is not prudery but the exact
opposite.   Purity is the power to see the
beautiful in all things and all functions of life,
and to glorify all actions by the spirit of un-

selfishness.   He who has learnt to be unselfish in every act of his sexual life, is pure. . . ." Here followed some instructions which could only prove elevating to mankind, but which prudish conventions do not allow me to publish. . . ."

". . . If *only* the pure in heart, in the sense of the sexually abstinent, could see God, then every old lady and old gentleman who had outgrown all their passions—or never had any— might be in that enviable position.   Why should God create in men and women a function by means of which they were to be debarred from seeing Him?   Maya again—even texts the unwary interpret through the veils of Illusion."

The Master then passed on to the wrong attitude towards love and passion adopted by some students and teachers of mystical or occult philosophy.   "You have no right," he declared, "to expect unadvanced souls to behave like advanced ones.   Though the example is trite, the child in the Kindergarten cannot be expected to know or learn the lessons of the Sixth Form. Nor must you expect even advanced souls to behave like perfect souls—there are only about three hundred *perfect* souls in this world—for even advanced souls may not be equally evolved

in all directions : there is a little chip out of the
crystal somewhere.   There is also the type of
body to be considered, in which an advanced
soul finds itself during a particular incarnation.
Take for instance the creative artist: very often
the finest creative artists appear by their behaviour in the domain of sexual morals to be
unadvanced souls.   And yet they are not—they
are merely born with a type of body which is
exceedingly difficult to operate and control.
When, say, a musician is composing a music-
drama or a symphony, tremendous forces from
Beings perceptible to clairvoyants are playing
around and through that man, and the result is
a stirring-up of his entire emotional nature.
Again—you have to realise that every form of
control entails the expenditure of force, and if
we consider that nearly all the force which the
creative artist has at his disposal must go into
his work, there is very little over by means of
which to control his sex-nature.   But even so,
the love-affairs of a great artist, looked at from
the standpoint of the Masters—who can *see*—
are not quite the same as are those of the
ordinary man.   Their very transience, which
the strict moralist condemns, is symptomatic not
of a vaccillating soul, but of a soul so one-pointed

that even love in its erotic sense makes no lasting impression on it.   It is only an evolved soul who can fall in love with ten women and not wish to marry any one of them.   The great artist knows, be it consciously or sub-consciously, that his love-affairs are only Maya—and as soon as anyone realises that Maya *is* Maya, he proves himself free from the thraldom of Maya.   Those self-righteous ones who exclaim: 'He's a genius, poor fellow, so I suppose we must forgive him. . . .' are neither charitable nor enlightened : only in the heart of the flower of true understanding is hidden the sweet honey of pardon.   Thus love-affairs are not evil in themselves; they are only evil when they upset a man's judgment, bring suffering to others or lure us away from the Great Purpose."

This statement, however, he went on to say, was not applicable to souls so advanced as to be nearing Masterhood.   In the case of these, sexual fidelity to one woman was desirable, because infidelity had a disintegrating effect upon the higher bodies.   Here M.H. gave a lengthy occult explanation which would not be intelligible to the uninitiated.

¹ Those finer bodies which surround and interpenetrate the physical, and are perceptible to the trained clairvoyant.

He concluded his discourse by saying : " The highest type of love may be seen where two people are united in the spirit of perfect freedom, yet neither of them feel the desire to avail themselves of it.   But although this may be the highest form of love, it is not of necessity the highest form of marriage.   Only when such people marry in order to serve the Higher Ones and Humanity, be it either through work which can only be undertaken conjointly, or by providing suitable bodies for souls wishing to reincarnate through them, only then do they enter upon that type of marriage which is the highest of all, and hence totally beyond the glamourous distortions of Maya."

CHAPTER XV

THE following Wednesday Master gave a lecture for the benefit of the newer *chelas* on concentration, meditation, and contemplation, and how by their practice permanent love-consciousness could be acquired. He told us that those who could succeed in holding their minds unwaveringly for eighty-four and a third minutes on the One Self, which is Unity—Love—Bliss, would retain those attributes of that Self as a consciousness for the remainder of their lives. But he warned us that such concentration was not only very difficult to acquire, but that long protracted meditation was injurious unless practised under the personal supervision of a Guru.

" Let people meditate often," he explained, " but only for short periods at a time. It is better to meditate say, ten times a day for a few moments or even less, than a whole hour in succession. And always remember," he added, "that the Imagination should be employed and not the *Will*, as most people understand that word; and further, that whenever we in this Order use the expression *to will*, we mean to make an effort of the imagination. Another important point is the necessity for synchronisation between feeling and thought. When you meditate on Love, you must not only think Love, but feel Love—again through an effort of the Imagination."

And here he pronounced one of those melodious utterances which remain in the foreground of memory.

"Imagination," he said, "is that divine ladder built by God, whereby the aspirant may climb to the blissful heights of Realisation.

"Those who indulge in mere desultory dreaming are misusing the faculty of imagination," he continued, "but if you who have recently become *chelas* will for the present practise meditation in the manner I have just advocated, you may eventually find that there will be times when you will be rewarded with a changeless feeling of love towards *everybody*, whoever and whatever they are, and yet you won't mind if they love you in return or not.

At such times there will be no more of those inconvenient antipathies you so often feel towards people ; you won't mind whether a person is ugly or beautiful, refined or vulgar, clever or stupid, wicked or virtuous—none of these attributes will inhibit the incomparable sensation of love flowing out in all its joy and peacefulness from yourselves towards them.   Some of you may even discover that such Love-consciousness has become permanent, for you may be only re-acquiring what you have already acquired in a previous life."

And he went on to show how even spiritual powers are dependent on past incarnations, the particular type of body we inhabit, heredity, and so forth.

As he neared the conclusion of his discourse he said : " Are there no other methods for acquiring this attitude of love—for remember it *is* an attitude—other than the methods of meditation prescribed ?   Personally I believe there are.   Take the analogy of the blacksmith's arm : his right arm is unusually strong and muscular, his left is weak and puny in comparison.   Why is this ?   Because he has developed the strength of his right arm by swinging the hammer ; his left he has only used as all people

use it who are not ambidexterous.   And it's
just the same with love—exercise the *will* to
love, and you develop the capacity to love, so
that your whole love-nature becomes strong and
enduring ; love in the ordinary way as people
do who are merely attracted, and your love-
nature remains weak and sickly, and eventually
dies altogether.   For observe : love requires to
be nourished *from within* and not from without.
As long as you are dependent on externals you'll
never be safe.   Only when you make up your
mind not to depend on those externals will you
be secure.   But you must start now while you're
young ; when you are old it will be too late.
The attitude once acquired will persist of its
own accord ; then when old age has come upon
you there will be none of this difficulty about
making new friends that we so often hear of.
Instead of merely being fond of one or two
friends you'll be fond of ten friends, twenty, a
hundred—there is no limit beyond what you
yourselves impose.   And of course as the number
increases the likelihood of your outliving them
diminishes.   The lonely lovelessness of old age
is but the penalty one pays for exclusiveness.

   " To come to a practical suggestion : why not
select at least one person from among your ac-

quaintances who is not sympathetic to you, and then, always, of course, with the aid of Imagination, *will* yourself to love that person.   I'm not by this implying that there are some here who actually and actively hate anybody, because, as you know, we dare not initiate those who have not got over such an emotion as hatred.   But there are still persons to whom you feel—shall we say extremely indifferent ; whose actual bodies are not sympathetic to you, so that you would not care to take their arm or touch their hand or show any of that physical demonstrativeness which especially women are accustomed to show one another.   You needn't even go further afield than our own immediate circle ; for although I admit that on the whole the spirit amongst you is one of love and fellowship, there is in some isolated cases room for improvement.   There are one or two or you women who might feel a great deal more loving towards each other than you do at present.   Your own hearts will tell you what I myself don't need to tell you.   But I ask you to let those hearts of yours speak, and to follow their promptings.   I assure you that by acting on my suggestion you can progress very considerably.   I should add that the exercise of this *will* to love need not

be restricted to members of the same sex. How
often, for instance, does a woman feel that such
and such a man is quite agreeable to talk to,
but that she would scream—women are very
fond of this talk about screaming—if he were
to take her hand or put his arm round her?
And the same with a man towards a woman,
except that men don't usually scream! Is any
form of repulsion, towards whomever it may be,
an ideal state of things? Oh, I grant I'm not
asking from you something that's very easy
when I suggest that you should overcome all
such repulsions—but then if we only did the
easy things in life we should never progress at
all. This love-consciousness at which you are
aiming has, like the kingdom of heaven, to be
taken by force ; to be conquered ; and like all
things where conquest is involved it requires
effort. I'll go so far as to say that it would—
for some people—be much easier to love God
than an unsympathetic neighbour. God you
can endow with every lovable and wonderful
quality you like, and He doesn't suddenly appear
in person to annoy and disappoint you. You
can even credit Him with undesirable qualities,
such as jealousy, anger, or revengefulness, if
these attributes happen to please you—but your

unsympathetic neighbour you're obliged to take just as he is. It is *you* who have to change, not he—and it is you who first of all must wish to change.

"And so I say to you who are striving for Love-conciousness, use every means in your power to attain it. Don't let mere meditation suffice, but learn to love even your seemingly less lovable neighbour. Learn to love him for the sake of the Self, the One in the Many."

CHAPTER XVI

THE REVELATION

BEFORE I returned to my club after the discourse
M.H. took me aside and asked me to come the
following Friday morning at eleven o'clock, as
he had something of importance to say to me.
That it was connected with what I had come to
think of as *the mystery*, I felt instinctively the
moment he spoke.   At last my countless speculations would be set at rest ; the time was now
evidently ripe for me to learn the reason for my
long journey.   But what had brought about its
ripening ?   Or better said, what actions on my
part had caused it to ripen?   This I was unable
to tell, and found the problem more baffling than
ever.   When I came to take a retrospective
view of past events, all I could see was my
romance with Clare and my friendship with

Viola Brind. I had of course in addition learnt much from Master's talks, but I was unable to connect anything in the nature of an intended sacrifice on my part with views and doctrines he had set forth.

I found the Master in an unusually serious mood when I walked into his study. Not that by serious I would imply even a suspicion of gloominess; I mean purely that the calm, benign, and fatherly attributes of his many-sided personality were more especially in evidence that morning.

" Let's have a smoke while we talk," he said, offering me a cigar after we had shaken hands.

I accepted one, and sat down in the comfortable armchair he had drawn up for me in front of the log fire.

"You will remember, my son," he began, "that when I wrote and asked you to come over here, it was with a definite object. This object I promised to make known to you in due course."

I nodded.

"Well, I think," he continued, " I may now tell you what I had in my mind. You are at a certain stage of your evolution and you'll perhaps remember I wrote you that unless a definite step were taken, I did not see the possibility of your progressing much further in this incarnation. You remember ? "

"Certainly I do."

" I'm going to ask you, my son, something which will mean an alteration in your whole life and which, as I've already told you, will demand great self-abnegation and even a reversal of some of your most cherished ideas.   But I hope and think that your faith is strong enough to make you realise that in doing so I have not only your evolution, but also your happiness in view.   Yes, a happiness so great that even you with your poetical imagination can only dimly conjure it up for yourself.   It's true you've already had moments of that Bliss-Consciousness at which all our students are aiming, but these have only made you long all the more to have that state more frequently.   Isn't that so ? "

" Absolutely."

" Well, now, as I said the other night, there are more ways than one of arriving at it.   There is the method of meditation which you are already practising, but there is also another—a quicker and more heroic method.   It is to place oneself in such circumstances that one is forced to will oneself to acquire that unconditional Joy-

and-Love-Consciousness—or else suffer in consequence."

"But how does one make such conditions?" I asked, utterly bewildered.

"That, my son, you *could* have gathered from our talks. But it is one thing to tell you all in a body, and another to ask you individually to carry out my suggestions. There are in fact *very* few here in this circle whom I could ask what I'm going to ask of you ; they are not all at the stage of evolution which makes such a test possible."

"But won't you tell me what it is?" I said, finding the suspense painful.

"All in good time, though I will not keep you in suspense much longer now." He paused for a moment, then continued : "You are approaching fifty, aren't you?—and up till now have not gone through an experience I regard as very beneficial to certain types of souls. That experience, my son, is marriage, for it is not good for a man to live his entire life alone, having to consider nobody but himself."

In a flash it came to me that he wished me to marry Clare, but my astonishment was so great that I cannot pretend to know whether I felt glad or sorry.

" You, my son, are averse to marriage ; you
do not believe in marriage, because you realise
that only in about one case in a thousand, if
even that, love endures and marriage turns out
a success ? "

" Yes, these are my views."

" But do you think any sort of aversion,
especially one so strong, is good for the soul—
does it not stand in the way of Advancement ?
Besides think how much can be learnt in the
process of trying to overcome that aversion, as
I pointed out only the other day."

" Then you wish me ... to marry ... Clare ?"
I stammered.

He shook his head gravely.   " That would
practically be marrying for your pleasure. You
love Clare—by marrying her the lesson would
be an easy one to learn."

" But I—I don't understand," I interrupted,
distinctly upset, " who else . . ."

" Listen, my son," he said soothingly, " unconditional Love-Consciousness is not attained
by loving somebody we already love, but only
by learning to love somebody we do not love as
yet."

" But surely," I exclaimed, " one can do that
without marrying them ? "

"One *can*, but one doesn't," he answered. " Then there are other reasons connected with the past ; Karmic reasons. And even that is not all in *your* case—I have still weightier motives for asking you to marry—a particular person—whom as *yet* you do not love."

Then suddenly with a shock I realised everything. " It's Viola Brind you mean ? " I said, making an effort to hide my feelings.

" Yes : it *is* Viola Brind."

For a moment, finding no words, I gazed dejectedly into the fire. It seemed as if he had asked more of me than I *could* possibly fulfil— yet at the same time I knew I should not refuse him. In those few moments I saw myself giving up Clare, with all the sorrow such a course would involve—and then tieing myself to a girl I now realised more than ever I did not love in the very least ; indeed the unaccountable feeling of antagonism towards her that had troubled me several times, now became suddenly enhanced to a formidable extent. I felt the idea of marriage with her absolutely repugnant, and almost resented that M.H. should demand such a thing of me at all.

His voice broke in upon my reflections—it sounded inexpressibly tender. " My son," he

said, touching my hand, " I'm sorry you should
suffer, but console yourself a little with the
thought that had it not been for your unflinching
faith and obedience I could never have put you
to such a test.   Even now—remember, I *force*
none of my pupils to do what is against their
will—they are all free agents and must work
out their own salvation.   You don't need to
give me your answer now ; I'd rather you did
not, for it's advisable you should have time to
reflect.   At present the idea is so new that it
not unnaturally startles you ; but believe me, it's
remarkable how soon one can accustom oneself
to even the strangest things.   Take your time,
think well over the whole matter, and then
choose.   In the meanwhile unburden yourself
fully to me, and ask anything that's in your mind."

" You mean ask you now ? " I said.

" Yes, my son ; I have specially made myself
free so that we should have plenty of time together."

I was silent for a moment ; my mind was in
such a state of confusion and I had so many
things to ask that I hardly knew where to begin.

"But what about Viola herself?" I said at last.

" She will agree if you do."

" Poor girl," I mused with a touch of bitter-

ness, "and she loves someone else . . ." Then
suddenly : " I suppose you mean it to be a
platonic marriage ? "

"No, my son, I mean you to be married in
every sense of the word."

I looked at him aghast. " But the idea is
horrible," I cried, " I don't think I could . . ."

" It may repel you at first, I grant—but not
so later on. And just think what you can learn
in overcoming that repulsion. Besides there
are other reasons why you should overcome it.
There is a particular ego for whom you two
could provide a vehicle ; this ego is so highly
evolved that he cannot reincarnate as the result
of passion, but only as the result of self-sacrifice
and deliberation. Vehicles produced through
passion may be all very well for medium souls,
but great souls cannot be brought into the world
in that way."

I sunk my head in my hands.

" Isn't it reasonable, my son," he continued,
"that advanced souls, as you two are, should
provide bodies for other advanced souls? How
could these obtain suitable vehicles at all if you,
and others like you, refuse to do your duty ? "

I was still silent.

Though he had put forward these same ideas

in his discourse on " Maya " the other night,
and I had given full mental assent to them,
it was, as he evidently realised, a very different
matter to be asked to put them into practice
myself.

" There is something further I must tell you.
Between you and Viola, some Karma has to be
worked off.   Do you know why that feeling of
hostility towards her came into your consciousness ?   It was because of misdeeds in the past.
My son, if you don't make good in this incarnation, you'll have to do so in the next—it
will only mean postponement.   You may resent
what I'm asking you to do, but it's not my fault
that your Karma has to be paid off, is it ? "

I seized his hand and pressed it by way of
answer.

" And then there is the work," he explained.
" You'll remember I told you that if you carried
out my programme, your inspiration would be
greatly enhanced.   And isn't that natural ?
Think what the poetry of a man would be
like whose consciousness was coloured with
Love and Bliss !   Would he not over-reach all
the poets of his day ?   But in addition to all
that, Viola, with her particular type of vision,
could help you in a way you little dream of.

She can *see* the other planes and give you first-
hand knowledge it would be difficulty for you
otherwise to obtain.   Also she will at times be
able to establish the means of communication
between yourself and me ; for it is not my wish
that you should permanently remain here.   It
is not the right atmosphere for you—besides, I
have work for you to do over in England.
You too must do a little teaching."

I was beginning to see things in a slightly
less gloomy light.   " You said once that I could
help *her*—but *how* ? "

" My son, you have more of the wisdom-side
of evolution than she has, and it will be your
mission to teach her what she lacks, for with all
her faculties she is not quite such an old soul as
you are yourself.   It will be the combination of
your wisdom with her intuition which will provide the suitable magnetism in which the
Masters can work through you both.   By living
together there will result an interblending of
atmospheres, so to speak, and that is why
marriage for you and Viola is so important."

I was silent again, though I felt less miserable
now that he had explained so much.

" Is there anything further you wish to ask,
my son ? " he said.

"What about—Clare? I am in love—even passionately in love with her."

He smiled at me cryptically. "Do not worry, my son. Viola will not be jealous, I think; nor is she asking you to give up Clare—all will smooth itself out in good time."

"Oh, I'm not one of those who think that sort of love lasts forever—I know it doesn't; but even so, how can I be certain that I shan't feel attracted towards other women?" I got out of my armchair and started walking up and down.

"Nobody is asking you to be certain. On the contrary it is for you and Viola to show to the world the ideal marriage of the future.—the free marriage which is beyond jealousy and acquisitiveness."

"But surely that's easy enough if one doesn't love one another?"

"You are forgetting what I've said, my son: I don't say you'll ever have a passion for each other, nor is that desirable; passion after all is only a form of bondage. You will, I think, overcome your physical antipathy, but that is different from feeling passion. What I foresee for you is a spiritual and mental unity, a perfect comradeship in every sense of the word, and with it, of course, perfect freedom; for true love knows no bondage nor jealousy. I daresay you know the original meaning of 'jealous' was 'watchful,'" he added parenthetically. "So you see you have no need to fear for your freedom. Just as you will not be jealous if Viola gets attracted towards other men, so she will not be jealous if you get attracted towards other women. Nobody has the right to hold a person exclusively to themselves—that is what I'm trying to teach my pupils over here, and that is why I often allude to it in my talks. I want my pupils to spread the ideal of the higher type of marriage and the higher type of constancy."

"That won't be very easy to teach a world that only understands enforced constancy."

"Or all-absorbing constancy," he added, which is not the ideal either, for it may lead to a kind of double selfishness. It is right that two people should possess a deep and beautiful devotion for one another, but it is not right that they should be so wrapped up, each in each, that no love is left over for anybody else. When this is the case, how can they hope to do good in this world through helping their fellows? Will they even *want* to help them unless they love them? For the spirit of service begins,

with love.   And so what I foresee for you and
Viola is not a selfish mutually absorbing love,
but that you should be help-mates one to the
other—unified in love and spirit, but free
nevertheless.   On the higher planes there is
already unity between you, but for Karmic
reasons it has not filtered through into the
physical as yet . . . And now is there anything
more you wish to ask me, my son?"

"I can't think of anything more at present,"
I answered.

"Very well, then.   Think it all over—and
may you choose wisely.   In the meantime do
your best to think of Viola with affection.   Use
meditation and suggestion for this purpose—
they will help."

"I will try," I said somewhat doubtfully.

"*And*—succeed . . ." he completed.

I prepared to take my leave.   He held my
hand for a few moments as we said good-bye.
"By the way," he observed, "I'm very glad you
took my advice and did not neglect your work—
you have turned the love which you are feeling
to good account.   If you will also try to express
in poetry your present turmoil of soul, you will
not only obtain relief but do good.   To you as
poet it is given to idealise suffering, and to give

its fruits to the world. Never forget that—and be grateful that it lies in your power to do so. The ordinary man rejoices or suffers, as the case may be—but who else benefits by his joy or his suffering? With you it is different; therefore see, my son, that you take advantage of that difference. And let it be a consolation to you to feel that from your sorrow others may reap good. I give you my blessing," he added, embracing me.

CHAPTER XVII

CONSEQUENCES

My first inclination on leaving the Master's house was to go straight to Clare for comfort. But as I was not certain whether I should find her at home, I thought it best to go back to the club and telephone to her. As I entered the hall, and from mere habit looked at the letter-rack, I found a note for me. Hardly looking at the envelope—I was too preoccupied with my thoughts to notice anything—I opened it and read :

" Dear Fellow-Chela,

My father has arrived in New York on business, so I am joining him there for a week or ten days. By now you will *know*. Master told *me* yesterday. I am dreadfully sorry for you and hardly know what to say. I am sure you must be wishing you had never set eyes on me. Still—if it *has* to be, I want you to realise that I will try my very best not to make it *too* hard for you. It is indeed a queer state of affairs that two people should have to try and comfort one another for having to marry one another, but if we *do* try, perhaps that will be the first step towards what Master wishes. I can't write more now, I only decided at the last moment to write at all.

Yours,

Viola Brind."

At any rate, I thought as I stuffed the letter into my pocket, *she* has broken the ice : our first interview in these extraordinary circumstances won't be quite so embarrassing *now.* Then I rang up Clare. She answered in person.

" I want to see you at once," I said.

" Yes, dear—is anything wrong ? Your voice sounds so strange."

" I'm rather upset—about something . . ."

" Oh, my poor honey ! Come right now and stay to lunch. Mother has gone to Brooklyn and won't be back till evening, I guess."

Ten minutes later I entered her boudoir.

" But what *has* happened ? " she cried, embracing me, "you look very badly—you're all drawn and queer-looking."

I sank down beside her on the sofa and leant my head against her shoulder. She took my hand in both of hers. " Honey—*what* is it ? "

"Something which sounds almost incredible. I can hardly believe it myself—yet."

"You've lost somebody?"

"Oh, no—not that."

"Well, then—what?"

"Master wants me to get married," I blurted out.

She started perceptibly. "Married! But—"

"Alas, not to you, darling. I wish to God it were . . ."

Though I could not see her face I knew by the way she breathed that she was undergoing a shock.

"You poor thing," she murmured after a moment's silence. "But I don't understand—is there some girl you've got into trouble?"

"Good *Lord*, no!" I exclaimed, lifting my head.

"Then for heaven's sake *why?*"

"Oh, it's a long story," I said wearily, "and you'll need every ounce of your faith to understand it."

"Are you absolutely forced to do it? Suppose you said 'no'?"

"In the circumstances I should be a fool to say 'no'—he says it would mean practically no more progress in this incarnation."

"It's all beyond me," she sighed with a gesture of bewilderment.

I then proceeded to tell her about my interview with M. H., and everything he had said. She listened with increasing amazement. "At any rate whatever happens, it needn't make any difference to *us*," I ended.

She shook her head despondently. "I'm afraid it *will* make a difference though."

"But why?" I cried.

"An engaged man . . . it's not the same— we oughtn't to see each other any more."

"Are you going to make it more difficult for me than it is already?" I asked sadly.

She was silent.

"Are you?" I persisted.

"There's Viola to be considered—she's my friend."

"But *surely* you don't suppose she will mind?"

"Women are funny—you never know."

"But even Master himself didn't say we were to break with one another!"

The gong for luncheon sounded, and I cursed the interruption.

"Clare!" I exclaimed desperately, "I'm about as miserable as any man can be as it is, but if

I've got to lose you as well . . .   For God's
sake say it's all right before we go downstairs."

She shrugged her shoulder.   "At least give
me time," she said in a hard voice, "at present
I don't know where I am . . . "

She led the way to the dining-room.   Over
luncheon, for which I had no appetite, it was of
course impossible to discuss the subject further ;
and as I was in no mood for other subjects, the
atmosphere was strained.   Clare made conversation of a sort, but it only jarred on me and made
me wish for silence, so that I might be left to my
conflicting thoughts.   What troubled me in
addition to everything else was pity for Clare.
The thought of hurting *her* was like a knife
stabbing me.   If I could make her understand
and view the situation as I viewed it, then all
would be comparatively well for us both, *unless*—
Suddenly it occurred to me that I had forgotten
to ask *when* Master wished me to go through
with this marriage.   Was it to be soon while I
was still in love with Clare, or would he be con-
tent if I waited a year, two years—how long ?
He had said that matters between Clare and
myself would smooth themselves out ; but what
did that mean ?   Why had it not occurred to me
to ask him to be more explicit on such an im-

portant point? I would certainly ask him to-night after the lecture; I must know at once, and so, I felt, must Clare.

Although after lunch we discussed the subject for nearly two hours, and probably would have continued longer if she had not had an appointment, we got no further. It was evident that with all her unconventionality Clare entertained scruples. She told me in so many words that to go on conducting a love affair with an engaged or married man was highly undignified and no the right thing.

"If you have to go through with this almost at once," she said, and her voice was still hard, "then we must make up our minds to separate; but if it's only in a year's time—well—I suppose you'll be long since back in England and—and we shall be separated anyway." And at that we left it for the time being.

I managed to get in a few words with M. H. that evening, though they were hurried ones, as he was leaving by a night train on one of his mysterious journeys.

"How soon do you want me to—to get married?" I asked, "you don't wish it at once, do you?"

"That would hardly be possible, my son," he

answered kindly, "for many reasons it can only be when you both return to England."

"I ask because of Clare—she thinks——" I hesitated.

"Well, my son, what is it?"

"That she ought to break off with me, if I . . . get definitely engaged."

"She too has her tests to go through and certain Karma to work off. What she may decide to do is not for me to dictate. Neither of you are children." He smiled gravely. "This is a matter which can only be adjusted between yourselves."

"Yet even foreseeing this you encouraged us . . . ?"

"To sympathise with those who are destined to go through a romance is not of necessity to encourage it. As I said, the Karma that is to be, *must* be. My work is to turn the outcome to good account. The only thing I'd suggest is for her to weigh her scruples and see if they stand the test of true unselfishness."

So Clare is also undergoing a test! I thought as I walked back to my club. It was too late to go and see her or ring her up, thus I was unable to relieve her mind about my marriage until the following day. On that day I did, however, after much difficulty and many tears on her part, manage to make her see the situation in a different light. And it was finally arranged that at any rate for the time being things should remain unchanged between us.

CHAPTER XVIII

ADAPTATION

MASTER remained away till the following Wednesday, so I did not see him again until the actual lecture; all the same I often felt him very near, as if he were inspiring me with encouragement and sympathy. In those few days I distinctly made some progress, though at times the feeling of antagonism towards Viola arose very strongly. But one thing I certainly did achieve: it was the resolution to go through with the project whatever might happen. I also wrote to Viola as nice a letter as I could manage to write, in which I told her the Master's wishes were law to me, as I gathered they were to her, and that I also would do all in my power to make things as little hard for her as I possibly could. I further asked her to let me know the moment she got back, so that we could meet and, as she suggested, "console each other for having to marry each other."

In reply she wrote telling me she would be back Thursday, the day after the lecture, and would I come to tea at her lodgings?

But of that I will write later, for the Master's lecture is what I am concerned with at this juncture.

"Well now—what's the subject to be this evening?" he asked as he stepped up on to the little platform. "Any suggestions?"

"Why not just *talk* and see what happens?" Arkwright said.

M.H. laughed, as did the others. "You'd better ask a woman to do that," he observed, "she'll talk to you about the philosophy of——"

"Hats—" said Heddon, drily, and there was more laughter.

"Thank you, my son, that reminds me of something that happened in England not long ago. You may or may not know that St. Paul once said no woman must enter a church with her head uncovered. As the result of this edict some clergymen made an outcry because a few women entered a church without their hats on. Those clergymen didn't seem to realise that in the days of St. Paul and in the country

where he lived, for a woman to enter a church—
or anywhere else for that matter—*unveiled*,
would be equivalent nowadays to her entering
a church in nothing but her underclothes."

Another outburst of laughter greeted this.

"Yes—it *is* funny," M.H. agreed, "it is also
instructive. It's even instructive enough to
provide us with a subject for this evening.
What would you say that subject *is?* I give
you three guesses."

"The philosophy of clothes, *à la* Sartor
Resartus," somebody suggested.

M.H. shook his head.

"St. Paul as Initiate," from Arkwright.

"Too obvious. Try something more subtle."

"Pin-points," * came the third shot.

"All wrong. The subject I had in my mind
was *Adaptation* : and by that I mean adaptation
of spiritual utterances, precepts and injunctions
to varying circumstances, nations and periods
of history. That episode I just related shows
on the part of those clergymen an unenlightened
attitude of mind. Far from it being a good
thing from *their* point of view for women to go
to church in hats, it would be much better to

---

* An expressive big of slang, practically untranslatable ; the
nearest approach to it being unessentials, "small-mindednesses."

pass an edict nowadays decreeing that all hats must be removed. Instead of attending to the service each woman may be, and probably *is*, either admiring, envying or criticising every hat within her range of vision.

"Well, then—It is obvious that every rule and religio-moral precept uttered two thousand years ago cannot be applied without the slightest alteration and adaptation nowadays when times and conditions have changed so materially. And I don't mind in what sacred book those precepts stand, nor who uttered them : it is all the same. Didn't Christ Himself tell the parable of the talent and the napkin, and censure the man for making no use whatever of his piece of money ? And yet that's exactly what so many people do with religio-moral precepts : they just leave them exactly as they stand, and don't adjust them to the altered circumstances of life."

The Master took out a cigar, felt in his pocket for matches, and not finding any asked for some.

" Smoking is also a matter of adaptation," he said after he had lighted up. " Perhaps some of you wonder why a man you believe to have bliss-consciousness *needs* to smoke. The answer is he doesn't. But he smokes all the same : he is adapting himself to you. If *I* didn't smoke

you'd feel uncomfortable when you wanted to
smoke yourselves.   This does not mean that I
am martyrising myself and that I dislike my
cigar—Oh no—because when we dislike a thing
we are doing we are not happy at that moment,
and of course there is no such thing as permanent Bliss-consciousness and unhappiness at the
same time ; black can never be white and Bliss
can never be its own absence.   But I have a
further reason for smoking—it is to make war
against what might so easily develop into occult
Pharisaism.   In some books on philosophy and
occultism I have seen statements which almost
imply that in order to reach Adeptship you must
act—well—practically like prigs.   These books
would have us believe that we must never laugh
heartily, that it's a dreadful and dirty habit to
smoke, that we ought never to drink tea or
coffee, never let a barber cut our hair, because
of the bad magnetism imparted by his hands to
our own precious head ; that when we go to a
restaurant we ought never to use the knives,
forks and spoons provided—also because of their
bad magnetism—but should take our own ;
further, that we should never eat uncooked food
unless we've picked it ourselves—again because
of the bad magnetism imparted to it by the

hands of the pickers ; and so on and so forth well-nigh *ad infinitum.* Now I don't for a moment say there's no truth in this matter of bad magnetism, but I *do* say that if you are such frail and sensitive creatures as to be materially affected by it, you won't get very far in this incarnation. To me the whole matter savours too much of the monastic conception of life. To prevent yourselves doing, seeing and coming into contact with this, that and the other, lock yourselves up in a monastery where you'll be safe. That is the idea I am constrained to see in this long string of prohibitions. Good gracious, is our progress along the path to be impeded by a puff of tobacco smoke or a bit of bad magnetism ; are we to be the slaves of mere trifling circumstances? If so, then our divine philosophy is indeed little use to us. Surely the very essence of that plilosophy lies in the word *immunity ;* it teaches us how *not* to be affected by the countless vicissitudes of life ; not how to *avoid* them by running away. And our philosophy teaches something more : it teaches us the art of *adaptation.* The true philosopher adapts himself to the exigences of life, not the exigences of life to himself.

" But we started with the intention of showing

the necessity for the adaptation of religious and moral precepts.   Have any of you a clear conception of the complete purpose of World Teachers ? "

" To emphasise different phases of spiritual ideals," somebody answered.

" And to adapt them to the needs of the times, you must add," corrected the Master. " that is why one World Teacher is not sufficient for all nations and all times.   He has of course other functions about which you will find a great deal of theorising in various occult books, but with these we are not concerned at present. One might put it even better still and say His office is to re-adjust the balance of moral and spiritual ideals.   The Masters have a similar office, but whereas each World Teacher does this on a very large scale, the Masters do it on a smaller one ; they do for their few pupils what the World Teacher does for mankind in general. The reason is obvious.   Those few pupils, through desiring to hasten on their evolution, are already now at a stage at which the generality of mankind will only arrive after a considerable period of time.   That does not of course imply that the World Teacher will have to wait before He appears again until *everybody* on this earth has reached so-called discipleship, but it does mean that the bulk of mankind will need to have progressed up to a certain point ; otherwise His advent would not be worth while. I said a moment ago that He comes to adjust the balance of moral and spiritual ideals. Let us take an example. We were talking of Karma one evening and showing that it could gain far too much importance in some people's minds. Now suppose the doctrine of Karma became as generally distorted as has been the doctrine of Faith in Christian countries—you know the nonsense that is preached, namely that by mere belief you can be immediately saved. What would the World Teacher need to do? He would have so to emphasise some other phase of religio-philosophical truth as to cause the idea of Karma to sink into the background. Only by so doing could He adjust the balance. The same would apply to morals. He will set new moral ideals for Humanity at large, just as we Masters, on a smaller scale, are setting new moral ideals for our *chelas*. Which reminds me that one of my pupils once wrote a book about my own humble self, though needless to say he used the utmost discretion and wrote it in a very veiled manner, otherwise," the Master assumed an expression of humorous solemnity, "there would have been trouble. In that book some of our views on the marriage question are set down, and I raised no objection to this as I was in hopes that they might do some good. There was a woman friend of my pupil's who was in great trouble and had turned to books on higher occultism for comfort ; and among many others he lent her was this anonymous one on myself. She read it ; and the next time my pupil went to see her I made it my business to be in touch with his consciousness as I wanted to assist him to help her. He himself wasn't aware of the fact, but that is neither here nor there. What concerns us is the significant verdict that good lady passed upon the book and upon me. ' Really,' she said, ' I'm *most* disappointed in that book you lent me about a Master. His ideas on love and on marriage—why—they're positively immoral ! If that's the sort of thing Masters teach —well...' The sentence was never completed."

This story told against himself raised a laugh all round.

"Perhaps you'll think," continued M.H. with a touch of mischief in his eyes, "that I sank through the floor when I heard this flattering opinion of myself—but no—I'm quite used to that sort of thing by now; I assure you my pupil felt far more uncomfortable than I did. And what do you suppose it was all about? I had merely pacified some irate parents who were behaving in a very small-minded fashion towards their grown-up children. I had persuaded a full-blooded military gentleman to forgive his wife and take her back instead of revenging himself in the usual way; and a few more trifles of that kind. In short, I had simply adapted the spirit of the last World Teacher's utterances to a few ticklish situations in our modern life. But because I had suggested the application of that spirit to a greater extent than is customary, I shocked that good lady and many others besides. You see, some people are as easily shocked by unusual virtues as by usual vices. It is the same with our religion : as long as we are mildly christian nobody objects, but as soon as we are unusually christian people think we're a bit touched. It's the feeling that to be different even in this respect from our fellows is not quite nice, not gentlemanlike, not ladylike. In the eyes of many persons to be unconventional is a crime. My own crime had consisted in suggesting an application of the Christ teaching which struck my pupil's friend as unconventional.

" People like that require to realise that books
even like the Bible, are in many ways similar
to those on medicine. In the Pharmacopœia
a countless variety of drugs are tabulated ; but
what would be the good of reading that encyclo-
pædic work unless one also learnt how to select
and apply and adapt those various drugs to each
particular complaint and patient? We Masters,
if we are anything at all, are spiritual physicians;
we endeavour to cure and nourish the souls of
our patients, not only by administering the
suitable spiritual drug, but by doing so at the
right moment. To this end it is essential that
we should possess a degree more knowledge,
insight, and imagination, than do the majority
of our fellows. But a *little* of that imagination
we *do* expect them to possess when they enter
upon the study which eventually will make
them as ourselves. Neither we nor the World
Teachers can dot every single *i*, just for the
benefit of mental sluggards. If people are so
lacking in imagination as not to realise that
when the World Teacher says, 'Forgive your
enemies' He also means forgive your sisters,
your brothers, and wives, is it to be wondered
at that we shock their susceptibilities in showing
how these ideals really *can* be carried to their

logical conclusion? Therefore I say—teach people Adaptation, teach people to ask themselves whether in all situations of life they are applying the spirit of charity and of tolerance, and you will teach them an invaluable lesson."

CHAPTER XIX

THE INTERVIEW

As a little boy I always imagined that the older one grew, the less was one troubled by such drawbacks as shyness, embarrassment, and the like—but I find this very far from correct. On occasions, even at my age, I am capable of feeling extremely embarrassed, and the prospect of my interview with Viola was one of them. It is true the way had been somewhat cleared by the exchange of letters, but even so I was full of speculations as to what I *should* say when it actually came to the point.

As it turned out, she spoke first.

"Well," she said with a wry smile as we shook hands, "we're thoroughly in the soup. The best thing is just to see the humour of it."

"Yes, I think that *is* about the best thing," I laughed, but my laugh sounded nervous. I also

noticed that she was nervous, despite her efforts
at concealment.

"I wonder if anybody in the world has ever
found themselves in such a curious situation
before," she said.

"Only in Court circles, I should imagine."

She looked at me enquiringly.

"Where a prince has to marry a foreign
princess for diplomatic reasons."

"Oh, that—I'm a bit dense to-day."

"I don't wonder at it—having to marry *me!*
I'm surprised you're not more than dense."

"But what about *your* having to marry *me?*"

"I'd much rather marry an advanced soul
whom Master thought a great deal of, than
take my chance with another woman."

"But you hate marriage itself, don't you?"

"How do you know that?" I was beginning
to lose my embarassment, "did *I* ever tell you?"

"No, but I know all the same."

"Clairvoyance?"

She shook her head. "Master told me."

My interest was immediately stimulated. "I
wonder if you felt as awful at *your* interview as
I did at mine!" I exclaimed, quite off my guard,
then realised that I had been very unflattering
to her—indirectly . . . I must have shown it by

my expression, for she laughed and said: "Oh, you needn't mind. I quite understand. I'm really awfully sorry for you."

"And I for *you*."

"At any rate I don't hate marriage itself like you do—women don't, you know."

"But it's rotten luck on you having to marry a man you don't love."

She hung her head and was silent for a moment. I felt she was thinking of the man she did love. "But I will get to love you," she said, shaking off her depression.

I suddenly drew back into myself: I did not want her to love me; I pictured her becoming sentimental, and the idea was repugnant to me. I felt that uncomfortable sensation of hostility again ; it gripped me and rendered me inarticulate. If only we could be allowed to remain platonic I should hardly have minded, but any other relationship—

She broke in upon my thoughts. "Did Master tell you what we did to each other in the past?"

"No. Merely that there *was* Karma to work off.

"Nor that we had been married before?"

"No."

"Well, we *have*—but we made a mess of it then ; twice, in fact."

"Then that accounts for what I told you the other day—the feeling of antagonism?"

"Yes, it *is* Karmic. In the life before the last you made me suffer—last life I made you suffer and you got to dislike me thoroughly."

"What did I do to you that life before last? Do you know or didn't he tell you?"

"You married me without really loving me—though you thought you loved me at first. You were a great student of philosophy—a sort of book-worm, and you wrapped yourself up in your studies and neglected me. I fell desperately in love with another man—I suppose as the result; but you locked me in a room and wouldn't let me see him. I believe I died of a broken heart or something of the kind."

"I sound a beauty!" I exclaimed, "no wonder I'm expected to make good. And the next life?"

"I made *you* fall in love with me ; and then when I got you, I threw you over for another man, and you got very ill and died young."

"Serve me right," I said, "did Master tell you all this?"

She nodded.

"What else did he tell you?"

"Oh—many things."

"Am I allowed to know?"

"I don't think he'd mind—at least most of them; but it's not easy for me to tell you—just now. When we get a little further—perhaps then."

There was a pause in which she offered me a cigarette and lit one herself. We smoked for a few moments in silence; then I said: "What I don't understand is if I made *you* suffer in one incarnation, and you made *me* suffer in the next, why aren't we quits?"

"Yes, I don't understand that either. We'd better ask M. H."

"How extraordinary it all is," I mused. "When I used to rack my brains to think what kind of a sacrifice I was intended to make, *this* certainly never entered my head."

"Nor mine . . . " her laugh was rather wistful.

"I suppose you wouldn't have married your man in any case?" I asked reflectively.

"You mean *he* wouldn't have married *me*? No, never."

"Nor would Clare have married *me*."

"Oh, yes, there's Clare—I'd forgotten her

for the moment. What on earth does she think about it all?"

"It's been a bit of a blow, I'm afraid. I want you to do something for me in that quarter—will you?"

"Well, of course."

"She has an idea that if you and I make up our minds to go through with this—even though it won't be for some time yet—*you* might object."

"*I* object? But for heaven's sake, why? Do *you* object to my still loving my man? How absurd! Poor old Clare . . . " she added affectionately.

"I wish you could make her see it."

"*Of course*, I'll make her see it."

"Thank you," I said, extending a grateful hand which she clasped. The feeling of antagonism had gone again, and I saw vistas of comradeship and mutual help.

We then turned to more mundane subjects—the prospective attitude of her parents, and also the financial side of the question. This latter I had feared might be an obstacle, for my creative activities were not money-producing. Although I was comfortably off for a bachelor, I would be *un*comfortably off for a married man. Viola told me, however, that

she had an income of her own and that she
would eventually inherit a good deal of money,
so that if anything I realised that my marrriage
would increase my fortunes rather than diminish
them.

It was nearly dinner time before I left her,
feeling that at any rate the strangest interview of my life lay behind me.   The one with
M.H. had been soul-disturbing and impressive ;
this had been of a very different nature, though
equally unique of its kind.

Months afterwards Viola fulfilled her promise
and told me more of *her* interview with the
Master.   It must have been as impressive as
my own on that memorable Friday morning,
and further goes to reveal the powers of the
Adept-mind.

He had been very paternal, very serious and
very gentle with her too.   Although she had
hidden her true feelings from me, and had
almost led me to believe that her aversion to
marriage with me was not so great as my
own to marriage with her, this was far from
the case.   She had told him that morning
that she really felt it impossible to make the
sacrifice he asked of her.   She was one of
those women who, far from having an aversion

to matrimony, regard a happy marriage almost as the one aim of a woman's life. To marry a man she loved had been her great desire ever since she was old enough to think of the subject at all.

"My child," he had said, "if you had been allowed to meet a man whom you could love as most people love when they wish to marry, where would your happiness have been when that love had worn off? There is one man you might have met and loved with all the passion of body and soul—*for a time;* but you were not permitted to meet that man for your own sake. Your ego forbade it, knowing it would be hostile to your progress, and ultimately, to your happiness. You married that man once before, but whereas you have evolved much, he has evolved but little, and would have resented your occult studies and stood in your way; finally you'd have come to see him as an obstacle and would have resented his interference, and then discord instead of continued happiness would have been between you."

She told me that once or twice during that interview she had broken down and sobbed, and that M.H. had taken her in his arms and soothed her as he had done with the girl in the churchyard.

"You see, my child," he had comforted her, "I can tell what lies ahead. What good would I be to you otherwise? I can see happiness in store for you if you will marry this man who I *know* will be your spiritual complement. He can help you more than anyone else, and *you* can help him. Will you not sacrifice your present dream of happiness not only for the sake of another's soul, but for the sake of your own *future* happiness? Come, my child, where is your selflessness of motive?"

"But it's awful to marry a mere stone when all my life I've longed for love," she had sobbed.

"My child, he who loses his life shall save it. I am not asking you to marry a stone: I am giving you a beautiful gem with many facets. Some of those facets shine, and some as yet do not. It is for you to polish those which do not, and make brighter those which already do. Yes, and there is even more to it than that: for if we don't polish a gem, the whole gem may become dull. Would you let this happen to one of my most precious sons?"

She had hung her head and made no reply.

"Listen, my child," he had proceeded, "though you are not given to expressing your enthusiasms so freely as some others do over here, yet you admired this man's work long before you ever met him ; isn't that so?"

She admitted this.

"You also know what *I* think of his work. Would you take away that man's chance of producing far greater work than he has hitherto produced, just for the sake of a dream which in this life you may never realise? For suppose you refuse to do what I ask, how can you be certain you'll ever meet a man you'll love and who'll love you as you now think you want to be loved? For the sake of an unrealisable dream are you going to deny the world the truly great works which, with all their elevating influence, could otherwise be given to it?"

"But how can such things depend on an insignificant creature like me?" she had asked despairingly.

"My child, even modesty must be tempered with discrimination. If one of the thousand links of a very long chain could speak, might it not say : 'How can the strength of this great chain depend on so small a thing as myself?' But he who can see the whole length of the

chain, instead of merely that one link, knows
the foolishness of that question."

"Can you also see," she had then asked
brokenly, "what will happen to me if—if I
can't bring myself to do this thing?"

"Yes, *that* I can also see," he had replied with
an indulgent smile. "When such an opportunity
has once been given, but has been rejected, a
feeling of dissatisfaction comes into and colours
the whole life; that dissatisfaction is, as it were,
the voice of the soul continually reminding the
personal self of what it has missed, and how
through thus missing it, it has wasted years and
years by the wayside instead of hastening forward towards the Goal."

It had ended in her promising at any rate to
try to view the matter in the light M.H. wished;
and I came to know later that she had written
that letter to me only one day after the interview
in order to force herself to keep her promise.
She knew that when the first step had been
taken, it would be far harder to turn back and
would mean humiliation. Nevertheless, she
told me that even after *our* interview she had
gone more than once to the Master and told
him that she really felt she could not go on
with it. But of this she said nothing to me at

the time, being gifted with the power of hiding her emotions. She did not want to hurt my feelings, also she was not at all certain of herself. Her feelings at that time—as is often the case with women—were strangely variable. One day she had fully made up her mind to do as Master wished, the next she felt it to be utterly impossible. It was only when he finally said she *must* choose one way or the other, that she at last decided—in favour of me.

CHAPTER XX

THE INVISIBLE CAUSES OF WAR

THE following Wednesday we were all assembled at the usual time, but there was no Master. Half an hour, an hour passed, and still he did not arrive. Yet I noticed no impatience, nor even especial surprise, except on the part of the newer *chelas*. These began to ask questions and to murmur something about getting home so late, having to be up so early in the morning—could M. H. have had an accident? Did anybody know where he could be? Did he often do this . . . ? And so on. I had asked several questions myself, only to be met with non-committal, though perfectly good-natured smiles or shrugs. Then I overheard Heddon answering someone : " He's in the Blue Room, where nobody's ever allowed to disturb him, and that's all I can tell you ! " So by this I knew at any rate that he

was in the house, and probably in *Samadhi;* *
but why he should choose to be in *Samadhi*
just then, I had no idea.

He appeared exactly two and a half hours
after time, and his first words were : " I thank
all my *chelas* who've been patient.   The others
—in case they should think unpunctuality
doesn't matter," he smiled, "well, it *does* matter
—to those who've not as yet learnt patience,
faith and control : that's why I'm so late."

As all this was said with a touch of humour,
though none the less meant to strike home,
most of us laughed.

"And now," he suggested more seriously,
"any of you who wish to go home may do
so, for the talk this evening will be a long
one.   I don't mind personally whether I get
to bed at all, but perhaps you'll say we are
not you.   Very good."

Nobody stirred.

He looked at us approvingly and said :
" Buddha maintained that the man who could
force himself to keep awake for two nights in
succession, might accomplish anything.   Very
well, let us start in by keeping awake for
half a night."

* Superconscious trance or profound contemplation.

The *chelas* laughed again.

But it is not the rather long discourse which followed that I intend to include in this book, but a shorter one which M.H. gave us in answer to a question.   He had ended his lecture with the sentence : "The man who fights his own character is a greater hero than the man who fights the most formidable foe, for the struggle between a man and his foe can last but a short while, but the struggle between a man and his own character lasts a whole life-time."

"You have just mentioned fighting," said Mr. Galais, "and I've often intended to ask you if you consider that humanity has evolved far enough to render another war impossible ? "

"No, my son," M.H. replied, and his voice was very grave, "humanity has *not* evolved far enough.   And we Masters already now can see those clouds forming which may burst into a storm even more frightful than the last. Instead of learning the lesson that the Great War had to teach, thousands of people not only shirked that lesson, but took advantage of the war to enrich themselves at the cost of the suffering of their poorer neighbours. Thus, and in many other ways, new Karma

was made where old Karma should have been
wiped off.   The type of peace that obtains
to-day, as all of you know without the telling,
is merely the cessation of fighting—the peace
of the letter but not of the spirit.   War has
been transferred from the plane of the visible
to the planes of the invisible,* merely to return
again to the visible in other forms—in strikes,
revolutions and general discordant emotional
turmoil.   And so it goes on in a vicious circle,
and more and more evil force accumulates;
the thunder-clouds on the unseen planes grow
larger and blacker.   Do you know that the
evil thought-forms generated as far back as
the days of the Gladiatorial Games, still persist?   Do you know that the thought-forms
created by Black Magic practised hundreds,
nay, thousands of years ago, are still to be
seen by those who *can* see?   Think, then, what
evil thought-forces the Russian Revolution with
all its cruelty and bloodshed must be creating
at this very moment.   What is to happen with
all that force?   It will gravitate by the law
of attraction to those other thought-forms just
mentioned, and will swell the storm-clouds yet
more.   No wonder the prophets lift up their

* But not invisible to Initiates and seers.

voice in warning !   The world *is* going through
one of its most critical periods of history, and
what we Masters fear for humanity is a conflict
between the Yellow Races and the White.   If
this should happen, God help you all.   Not
only will you have to contend against numbers
far outweighing your own, but with the terrible
cruelty which characterises insensitive fourth-
race bodies.   Should this war eventuate, then
the progress of the world will be thrown back
for thousands of years."

The Master paused, and there was a note
of appeal in his voice when he continued : " It
is for *you* to prevent this war—it is for those
all over the world *like* you to prevent it.   It
is for the members of mystical, occult, masonic,
New Thought and similar communities to
live up to the very highest in their nature,
and so help the White Powers to overcome
the Powers of Evil.   It is for you to generate
those spiritual forces which may be used ·by
the Great White Lodge to disperse the thunder-
clouds of impending war.   And if at any time
during the next years you see those signs
which might herald the approach of this great
war, or any other war, then is the time to
sink all thoughts of personal evolution into

the higher cause of saving humanity. Think Peace, visualise the word Peace in large white shining letters.   You who are Americans, visualise them in your Government House ; you who are Englishmen, in your Houses of Parliament, over the King's palace, and over the King himself. Because those who definitely work to serve the White Powers are in the minority, they must work double time, as it were, and put forward the maximum of effort. Teach Christians to think and feel peace in their hearts and *really* to love their enemies. Teach Christians not to hate war because they *fear* war, but to hate war because they love Peace in its highest and truest sense.   Only when mankind has learnt to feel 'Peace and Good-will towards all men' in their own hearts, will the danger of wars have passed, never to return."

CHAPTER XXI

THE DECISION

M.H. HAD given me an appointment for the following afternoon at tea-time. When I arrived I did not find him in that serious mood which had characterised the previous occasion.

"Well," he said cheerfully as I entered, "greetings to you, my son." He took my hand in his. "How do things stand *now*? Have you come to *ask* me something or to *tell* me something?"

"Both," I answered, "and I think you know it."

He smiled to himself by way of reply.

"I have decided—to do what you ask," I said.

"I am glad, my son, *very* glad," he spoke lovingly; the paternal element had come back into his voice.

" But there are things that puzzle me—"

" Ah—well, perhaps we can straighten them out for you."

"I don't want to sound conceited—but I think I may safely say I'm a fairly philosophical person as a rule; I *do* think I've actually imbibed a good deal of the right attitude towards life. Things have ceased to trouble me—I mean the kind of things which seem to upset others."

He had folded his arms and was looking at me intently as he listened.

" It's true," I continued, " that I've objected to marriage, because with my temperament I've been convinced that it wouldn't do. I've not been one of those who could see thousands of unhappy couples around me and imagine I'd be the one exception. But apart from that, I've always thought that marriage would be an obstacle to my work. I've believed in the doctrine that an artist should be wedded not to a woman but to his work. Besides, how could I hope to write good stuff with a young brat tooting on a tin trumpet or yelling at the top of his voice?" (M.H. laughed heartily). " Yet I knew that to marry and refuse to have any children wouldn't be right either. I've at least enough sympathy and understanding to realise

236 THE INITIATE IN THE NEW WORLD

that it's quite unfair to deny a woman what is
the greatest and most natural desire of her life.
Somebody once told me that marriage means
so much more to women than to men, because
of this intense, though often subconscious, long-
ing to have a child.   Is that true ? ''

He nodded.

"So you see, if I have an aversion to marriage,
it's not founded on mere caprice but on what
seems to me good sound common sense.   But
now comes the puzzling part of the whole business.   Although you've shown marriage to me
in quite a new light, and I'm convinced that all
you say about it is true, why on earth do I
suffer like this ?   When I think over the matter
with calm, cold reason, I can see very little to
be upset about.   It will only be more or less like
living with a friend, and as far as that goes, I've
lived with a friend more than once in my life,
and got on splendidly.   There is of course the
physical side, but after all it's not as if Viola
were an old lady or a hunch-back or even ugly.
I can imagine some people finding her extremely
prepossessing.   It seems to me, then, that my
suffering is quite out of proportion, and also
quite inconsistent with my general character and
philosophical attitude towards life.   So I ask

myself *why*—or rather I should say I've come to ask *you* why ? "

" The whole thing can be accounted for in one word—the *Blacks*," he said, handing me a cigar and taking one himself. " Don't you see, my son, that these brothers of the Left-Hand Path have everything to lose by this prospective marriage, and so they'll do all they can to prevent it ? They're perturbed enough about your work as it is, because of the good it will do when humanity is a little more ready for it ; but if through marriage that work becomes ten times more powerful, is it to be wondered at that they try to bring about your downfall ? "

" But can they succeed ? " I asked apprehensively.

" Not unless you allow them to. And remember you have the White Masters to help you.'

" There is another thing I want to ask you— it's about Karma."

" Well, my son ? "

" I understand from Viola that in one life I injured her, and in the next she injured me ; if that's so, why doesn't the Karma work out equal ? "

" Two wrongs hardly make a right, my son. If in your last life you had forgiven her for the

wrong she did you, it would have been different.
But when she threw you over, you allowed vanity
and resentment to get the upper hand, and so
your love turned to hostility.   Had it been
otherwise, in *this* incarnation you wouldn't have
had to wrestle with yourself as you have to now—
for you'd have loved her of your own accord."

"But what about the Blacks in that case?"

"They would have sought other means to
separate you—perhaps influenced her parents
against you, or something of that kind.   There
are more ways than one of making it uncomfortable for people."

"It seems incredible that I should be worth
all this trouble!"

"My son," he said lovingly, "we Masters are
not grudging with our praise and encouragement
where these are due; and so I will tell you without reserve that it's your absolute purity of
purpose which rejoices the White Masters but
angers the Black ones.   There are few people
in whom the spirit of service is so pronounced
as in you.   It was this which attracted the
Masters, and it was because of this our Chief
sent me to you in London—though of course
you were not aware of His part in it.   Yes, my
son, though many things may look like chance,

nothing is chance really, and you have to thank
your purity of heart that you and I ever met in
this life. And if before long you reach Bliss-
Consciousness, as I hope and think you will,
you'll again have to thank your own faith,
obedience and efforts. Therefore do your own
utmost to complete what you've so well begun.
And when the Brothers of the Left-Hand Path
raise up that wall between you and the woman
we have chosen to help you along the Path,
then simply call down the Love of the Masters
on her—and the wall will vanish. Do this each
time it happens, and one day it will happen no
more. And also, my son, take her hand sometimes and show other little marks of affection,
even though you do not feel inclined; and if
she does the same to you, do not shrink, but
accept it for the sake of the One Love—the
Unconditional Love Itself. Learn to come to
the personal through the impersonal. Hitherto
you have only loved those who have attracted
you, which after all is not very difficult; but
now you must learn to love someone who does
not attract you, and that can only be achieved
through the impersonal Love. And realise
that such Love, when once attained, can never
be destroyed by the Blacks, for they can only

work on the personal which belongs to the astral plane—the higher planes they can never touch . . . And now is there anything more you wish to ask me?"

"Yes—just one thing, it's a point about tests."

"Yes? What is troubling you on that score?"

"You said the other day that Clare had her tests too. I took your advice and told her what you suggested—I mean that she should look her scruples well in the face. I also told her that as long as I was still over here, I understood you to mean that this prospective marriage-project needn't be allowed to make any difference. Was I right?"

"Quite, my son."

"Well, I'm going to say something that may sound rather strange in the circumstances, because it would come very hard for me to give up Clare *at present*, so please don't misunderstand me. But wouldn't it be a far greater test for her if you *did* ask her to give me up now?"

He smiled indulgently, and his answer was—to *me*—profoundly instructive. "My son," he said, "that which appears on the surface to be the most painful does not always prove the most useful lesson in the end. Let me give you a very simple example. Supposing a woman—of

course I don't mean Clare herself in this case—
is both extremely proud and extremely conventional, and she falls in love with a man who
doesn't propose marriage to her, his reason being
that he feels he must get to know more of her
character before it would be wise to do so. Now
wouldn't that woman be learning far more by
overcoming her pride and her conventionality,
than by giving up that man, even if she were to
suffer in the process of giving him up?"

I began to see what he meant.

"Of course the world who couldn't look into
her soul would say she was perfectly right—and
so she might be from the conventional point of
view. Take your own case. If you were to tell,
not the wordly-minded person but someone who
already had spiritual ideals derived mostly from
books on ethics and theosophy—if you were to
tell someone that you were about to marry a
woman who didn't love you and whom you didn't
love, what answer would you get? You'd be told
that it was an immoral and disgusting thing to
enter into intimate relationships with anybody
unless you really loved them. And yet here am
I, one of the Elder Brothers, asking you to do
this very thing. Now do you understand? If
Clare could learn the particular lesson I think she

ought to learn by giving you up *now*, I should ask her to do so, but as *I* see her character I know that she can learn a greater lesson by not giving you up.   It is for me to judge, not for you, my son; and I am glad you followed my advice even if you didn't see its significance."

He got up from his chair, which I took to be a sign that I ought not to stay any longer.   But at the door he said, firmly grasping my hand: "I give you my blessing on the resolution you have made, my son."   And I went away feeling happier than I had done for some days.

CHAPTER XXII

SEX

It was shortly following this interview that M.H., after one of the Friday talks, made some illuminating remarks on the subject of sex and present-day sexual morals.

Viola had asked his opinion of psycho-analysis.

"This science," he replied, "is one which may and does prove highly beneficial in certain cases, such as where the neurosis is due to some impression received in early childhood, or at any rate *during the present life* of the patient. But as the majority of psycho-analytic practitioners do not admit the existence of anything beyond the material plane, and hence do not take into account man's higher bodies and the laws of Karma and reincarnation, they are to a great extent working in the dark, with forces which they do not truly comprehend, and thus playing with that little bit of knowledge which is so dangerous a thing.   For example, I once knew a case in which the analyst unknowingly probed so deep into the patient's subconscious mind, that memories of long past incarnations were uncovered, that should never have been touched in this present life at all.   As most of these memories were of a primitive and painful nature, shocking to the personality, the patient was overwhelmed with such a sense of guilt, remorse and self-abasement, that instead of that harmonization of the entire being which is the psychoanalyst's true aim, exactly the opposite was the result.

"But for what we have special reason to be grateful to Freud and other exponents of the science, is the manner in which they are gradually educating people to adopt a more rational attitude towards all matters of sex.   They are helping to dissipate that reprehensible feeling of disgust which has been brought over from the repressive epoch of Queen Victoria.   For the so-called 'chastity' of the Victorian era was only surface and not intrinsic chastity.   Octogenarians may recall with pride and satisfaction the beautiful innocence and purity of their young days, when every well-brought-up girl blushed when looked at and fainted when proposed to ; but just consider the different conditions of those days. There were no bicycles for women, no violent games, no health and muscle-producing contrivances ; merely such mild pursuits as croquet, embroidering, gossiping, piano-tinkling, and the like. No wonder girls were chaste, with such poor circulations ; no wonder they fainted and burst into tears on the slightest provocation, when their bodies were a mass of toxins as the result of inactivity. How easy to be chaste in such circumstances, and consequently how little meritorious, especially if you add to the foregoing the constant attendance of a governess, chaperon, lady's maid or any other kind of society spy you like to imagine. It was very much like being immured in a convent or shut up in a cage! But let the young nuns come out into the world, and let a few Adonises start making love to them, and then we'll see if they're really chaste or not. The criterion of virtue is not how people behave when they are bound, be it by the walls of a convent or the subtler walls of public opinion or social conventions, but how they behave when they are *free*.

" And the young people of to-day *are* free ; partly as an indirect effect of the war, and partly because, as I said, psycho-analysis has shown the evils of sexual repression, and consequently a fair proportion of parents and guardians have become more tolerant.   There are others, on the contrary, who are more than ever shocked and pained, and ask themselves what the young people are coming to, and wonder ' where it will all end . . .'   And these questions are to be expected from individuals who can only see, as it were, in terms of a few years, and even then merely the surface of things without their under-lying cause.   But we Masters who look at matters from the standpoint of centuries, regard the present sexual situation simply *as a necessary stage in evolution.*   To return to my simile of the nun and the convent.   It is easy for a nun to be chaste because she has neither temptations nor opportunities to be otherwise.   But suppose she were permitted to come forth into the world and be as unchaste as she liked without her Mother Superior or anyone else making objec-tions—what then ?   Only if *in spite of all her freedom, she chose to remain chaste*, would she really be living up to the ideal of chastity.   It is the motive which makes the merit.   The *motive* with which individuals can henceforth set out to learn chastity, is the pure aspiration to acquire control, and that alone.   As the social walls by which, so to speak, women have hitherto been enclosed, are for the most part knocked down, there is less fear of consequences, and hence the purely material reasons for chaste behaviour have practically vanished. Even the distorted idea that sex-passion is evil in itself or degrading or necessarily hostile to spiritual advancement, is losing its hold on public opinion. What reasons, then, are left, or better said, will be left, when the walls are completely laid low? None—except the reason which comes from *within :* this one desire for *control*, this one desire to be the masters of nature in all its branches, instead of its slaves."

The Master paused, then after a while continued : "And now as we are on the subject of sex, I should like to add a few words relating to sex-aberrations. These have, as you know, engaged the attention of the psycho-analyst, but only the occultist, I think, touches the root of the matter, and in so doing, helps to dispel the pronounced spirit of intolerance which is directed towards them. For strange though it may seem, sex-aberrations are not of necessity a sign of utter depravity ; they are often the result of an attempt on the part of the Higher Self to conquer sex-desire altogether. This is sometimes the case with those who have developed their mental body before their astral, or where the soul is, as it were, trying to progress too quickly for the unmanageable physical body which it inhabits. You may of course think that the method is a very peculiar one, yet it is more its manifestation on the physical plane which works out as peculiar, rather than the method itself. Let us take an example from Nature. Supposing you stand a board up on its side across a flowing stream, what happens? The water, prevented from taking its usual course, rushes off into numerous little side-streams, which may run for quite a distance in all directions. It is very much the same with the sex-force. The result of trying to damn it up, is that it goes off into a variety of side-channels which are apparently as far removed from normal sexuality as are the numerous little outflowing tributaries from the stream's ordinary course. And so if you can realise this fact when you come across people with sexual aberrations and teach others to realize it too, you will help mankind towards the attainment of a greater charitableness instead of that feeling of disgust, contempt and repulsion which they usually show towards abnormalities which they fail to understand. Of course as a rule the people themselves who are abnormal in this respect, do not realise what their egos are trying to accomplish, but that does not alter the fact itself. Here again, by the way, your own occult knowledge may prove of great help. I once heard of an unfortunate boy who committed suicide on account of one of these abnormalities. He was an idealist along spiritual lines and had been a monk in a previous incarnation. If someone with occult knowledge could have told him the reason underlying his sexual aberration, he could have been saved; for it was just the overwhelming shame occasioned by the conflict between his ideals and his desires which caused him to abandon his body.

"Again, these abnormalities are sometimes to be accounted for by the fact that the soul which in itself is sexless, inhabits on the physical plane a body either male or female; and if by chance a man has been a woman in his last incarnation, or *vice versa*, the tendency may be retained to repeat the sexual trend of that last life, regardless of the difference in the present physical body. Such persons cannot be cured by penal methods, but only by psycho-therapeutical treatment of a very specific kind.

"And so you see, even in a question like this, it is mainly a matter of looking deep enough ; and those who are in a position to do this, should help those who are not.   Knowledge is power, but never forget that that power should be used for others, and not for oneself.   The more highly evolved we grow, the more we can feel for the difficulties, vices and passions of our fellows. There are many would-be occultists and others who so completely overlook this, that they are even shocked that we Masters should enter into this question of sex-aberration at all.   They imagine we ought not to soil our lips by as much as talking about such things.   But alas, it is they who are at fault, and not *we*.   Can our lips be soiled through our love for 'the great orphan humanity,' as one of us has called it?   For remember, love which is not coupled with full understanding, is not love as *we* comprehend the fullest sense of that word.   And surely it is the function of real love to understand and sympathise with every phase of life, whatever it be : and especially such phases which entail pain and suffering to our loved ones."

CHAPTER XXIII

THE RATIONALE OF CLARE'S TEST

My stay had protracted itself until Christmas and I spent Christmas Day with the Delafields. In the evening they gave a party to which several friends were invited, including Viola.

It says much for Clare and the latter that the marriage-project, far from diminishing their friendship for one another, actually augmented it. They sought each other's society more than ever. Advanced souls that they were—could they have been M.H.'s pupils otherwise?—they exchanged sympathy, Clare with Viola for having to marry me, and Viola with Clare for having to *lose* me, not because of the marriage itself, but because of the separation which would inevitably come about before long. The end of my stay was now in sight, and Clare was beginning to dread the parting, as was I myself. Much

as we loved each other, we were both too enlightened to suppose that that kind of love
would survive the test of time and separation.
But to let our love gradually die, and to suppress
it at its height as Clare imagined we ought to
were two very different things; and that she
finally decided against the latter course I afterwards learnt was not so much due to *my* efforts
as to Viola's

I also came to know why the test imposed on
Clare by M.H. was not in the nature of asking
her to give me up: he desired to test her faith,
and further to make her realise what he himself
had impressed on me in our last interview. For
however unconventional Clare may appear to a
particular type of English mind, for an American
girl she was less so than it might seem on the
surface. There are a number of American
women who do not consider it wrong to allow
the men they love a certain license, provided
those men are neither engaged nor married.
As soon, therefore, as I became to all intents
and purposes engaged, Clare came up against a
streak of conventionality in her character which
the Master had seen but which I myself had
little suspected. She had pretended to me on
the occasion when we first discussed the matter

that Viola might be hurt if we continued to love one another; but it *was* only pretence, as even I surmised.

In one of the many discussions we had on the subject she said: "He seems to be asking me to do a thing which is actually wrong, and not only *me*—but all three of us."

"How so?" I asked.

"First of all he, well, allows you and me to love each other, then a few weeks later he goes and tells you to get engaged to Viola, and after you *are* engaged he tells you it is not necessary for me to give you up. Are you sure, dear, it isn't *you* who've got a bit muddled?"

"I'm perfectly sure."

"Well, then, I don't understand."

"Why don't you go and ask him yourself?"

"I'm a bit scared. Besides he might just say: 'You've had it from two people, isn't that enough?'"

"Then Viola has told you too?"

"M'mm . . .

"I wonder why you're shy with Master?" I said, "somehow you're not the same Clare when he's about. You even talk quite differently. You lose the little American turns of phrase I find so fascinating."

"You're a darling," she said, pressing my hand. "But am I really different?"

"Of course you are, and you know it."

She laughed. "But he's so wonderful and impressive and——"

"If he's so wonderful," I interrupted, "why do you doubt him?"

"I don't know. I don't want to doubt him, but he does ask us to do queer things, now doesn't he?"

Nevertheless it had ended in her passing the test, and on the strength of it, M.H. asked her to come and see him the day before Christmas.

"He was just lovely," she said, and I couldn't help laughing, even though I was getting accustomed to the phrase—many of the girls used it. "I *was* scared at first, but I think I've gotten over that for good now—I hope so, anyway."

"Am I allowed to hear what he said?"

"Surely, but it won't be the same thing—telling it."

"Never mind about that. Was he in a very serious mood?"

"Not at first. He saw I wasn't quite myself, and talked in a cheery sort of way."

"And afterwards?"

"He got more solemn, but *very* loving—always 'my child.' How little one gets to know him from his 'talks.'"

"But surely you saw something of the real man that day in the churchyard?"

"Yes, but you forget, after hearing him on Wednesday, he's so different then. He seems to have so many personalities. He was different *again* yesterday, though more like that time we took the trip together."

"Did he say much about *us* ?"

"Oh, a lot."

"What sort of things did he say ?"

"Nice things."

"Well—*tell* me."

"It's not easy to reel them off right now."

She finally did manage to give me a very fair impression of that interview, all the same. He had, in the first place, commended her for allowing faith to overcome doubt.

"My child," he had said, "without faith we can achieve nothing in life—we cannot even walk across the street."

She was puzzled; this sounded a little too far-fetched to be believed.

"Well, isn't it so?" he had continued, "would you ever set out to cross the street if

you hadn't sufficient faith to realise that you'd
get to the other side? That faith is based
on memory and experience, hence understanding, oh yes—but it *is* faith all the same. And
so, my child, if you would progress quickly,
never for an instant lose hold of your faith."

"But that sounds almost like ordinary
Christianity," she objected, thinking herself
quite bold in doing so.

"There are many things in ordinary Christianity which are not to be despised," he smiled
gravely, "and yet there is a difference. Some
preachers of Christianity see merit in trying
to believe the unbelievable—and that is called
'blind faith.' The faith which isn't blind is
based either on understanding alone or on
understanding coupled with imagination."

Again she was mystified. "When I decided
not to break with—Mr. Broadbent, I did so
even though I didn't understand."

"Then why did you do it, my child?" he
had asked very gently.

"Because *you* wanted me to, or so I thought."

"And wasn't that because your imagination
told you I had very good reasons for wanting
you to?"

"Yes—I suppose it was."

"Well, then, wouldn't it be correct to say that peculiar though I am, you have at any rate a partial understanding of me, and for the rest you fall back on the divine quality of imagination? The two together constitute your faith, and that is the faith by which you will progress."

He had paused for a moment, then added: "The man you love is a very dear son of mine—it *is* just his unswerving faith which makes him so dear to me and to the other Masters—you know that all Masters are one. Because of his faith he came over here, and because of his faith he will make this sacrifice I have asked of him."

"But how will it all end—for me, for *us?*" she asked suddenly.

Again he had smiled gravely, "If I were to tell my *chelas* exactly all that was in the future, I should be giving them an advantage over their fellow creatures which they have not earned. If I tell you it will not end in unhappiness, that is enough."

"Have we been together in other lives—I mean he and I?" she asked.

"Yes, my child"

"As what?"

"Oh—as brother and sister, as mother and son. *He* was your mother, last time."

She laughed. "That seems *very* strange. If that's true why did we fall in love in this life?"

"When two souls re-meet in bodies of the opposite sex, the physical often obtrudes itself— at first."

"Now I come to think of it, what you say about mother and son accounts for something— I always feel that Charlie's attitude towards me is extraordinarily protective."

"Your feeling is quite correct: there *is* a great deal of the paternal in his love. Even his poems—those which *you* have inspired—contain much of that element."

"You *really* think I've inspired him?"

"Certainly, my child."

"Oh, I'm so happy!" she cried.

"To artists, poets and musicians, love is the great source of inspiration. That is partly why some artists have so many love-affairs. The world grudgingly forgives the men, but their partners, the women, they do not forgive. Yet much should be forgiven the women too—for through their love for these men they have indirectly enriched the very world which condemns them"

"You are wonderfully charitable!" she had exclaimed, "do you know, sometimes I feel I want to—to kiss you . . ."

By way of answer he had taken her hand and kissed *it* instead.

"Do you think it was very forward of me? she asked me with one of her most child-like expressions.

"*He* evidently didn't think so."

"Wasn't it just lovely of him?"

I smiled. "You are the most adorable of children . . ." She was quite right, I did feel very paternal towards her—I was even becoming conscious that the paternal element was in the ascendant. My love was gradually undergoing a change: I loved her, but I was not quite so much *in* love with her. Was this what M.H. had meant when he said: "Don't worry, my son, things between you and Clare will smooth themselves out?"

CHAPTER XXIV

THE TYRANNY OF VIEW-POINTS

MASTER had left Boston late on Christmas Eve and did not return till the following Wednesday in time for the lecture.

" In that little book," he began, " I sometimes quote called 'the Real Tolerance,' it is stated that a point of view is a prophylactic against all evil : but whether that is true or not entirely depends upon what the point of view happens to be ; it can also act as a prophylactic against good as well as evil, and for that reason the adoption of a judicious view-point is one of the most important things in life.   Look around you and you'll see that the majority of people are the abject slaves of their view-points.   Because of their view-points, even so-called good persons will commit the most uncharitable atrocities on themselves and on others ; the religious fanatic will hold his arm in the air till it withers ; another

will make up his mind not to speak for a number
of years ; another will turn his daughter out of
the house because she's had an illegitimate child ;
a fourth will disinherit his only son because he's
married a barmaid ; a fifth will shoot his wife's
lover because he thinks his outraged honour
demands it ; a sixth will never wear a hat in the
street because he thinks it's good for the hair—
and so on it goes from the great to the small ;—
and all because of a point of view.

" I once read that book *The Garden of Allah*,
by Robert Hichens. It is an instructive story
because it shows how a good and loving-hearted
woman will, under the tyranny of a view-point,
behave in a hard and uncharitable way, thereby
torturing the man she loves and herself in addition. You remember the story—the book is a
popular one—how a woman who is an R.C.
meets a man in Egypt, falls deeply in love with
him and he with her, how without any attempt
to know one another's histories or characters
they rush to the altar, so to speak, and immediately afterwards make a long journey into the
desert where they live for a time in conjugal
bliss, and as the phrase goes, are all in all to
each other ; so much so that the man, at any
rate, would like to have his wife entirely to him-

self and resents the appearance of any strangers or acquaintances on the scene. Yet in spite of all their estatic love-making the woman has a feeling that her husband is not completely happy, and that something is preying on his mind, some secret he is afraid to reveal. And then finally matters come to a climax and she learns from his own lips that he is an escaped Trappist monk and has broken his vows after so long a period as twenty years. He had entered the Order when he was too young to realise the fireiness of his own temperament, and although all went well for a time there came a day when through a combination of circumstances, together with an insufficiency of insight on the part of the Head of the Monastery, he was able 'to resist everything except temptation,' and so at last had run away.

"And now, on hearing his confession, how does this woman behave? The first thing she does is to move into another tent. Not because she has ceased to love the man—oh, no—after an inward struggle with herself she comes to the conclusion that she loves him more than ever— all the same she moves into another tent because it strikes her as the proper thing to do. (In all matrimonial differences, the first thing is to move

out of the bedroom!) That the wretched man
is already suffering agonies of soul she knows
perfectly well, but this doesn't deter her from
adding to them by the course she adopts ; not
only does she refuse to share the same tent with
him, but she won't even touch his hand. Not
one comforting sisterly sign of affection will she
show to that unfortunate, misery-stricken husband of hers. On the contrary, she is outwardly
as adamant as a stone. And what is more,
having prayed to God, she imagines *He* is up-
holding her in her resolves.

"How does the story end? She, with the
supposed assistance of God, forces the man to
go and confess to a certain austere priest, who
she knows will prescribe but one course of
action—that her husband should go back to the
Monastery from which he has escaped. This
he does the very next day, and only as he is
about to enter the door, does she imprint one
little kiss on his forehead. She won't even
comfort the man by letting him know that she's
expecting a child to enliven her own loneliness
—not one fraction of an inch will she give
way. The final picture shows a garden on
the edge of the desert in which, with her little
son, she lives shut away from the world, and

dreaming of the husband she will never see again.

" Here then we have a story showing up with admirable consistency the tyranny of a viewpoint. Let us examine the matter closely and see what we can learn from it, and what in the nature of a warning we can extract. As the woman in question doesn't exist," the Master interpolated whimsically, "we shall not be guilty of uncharitable gossiping if we say exactly what we think about her.

"And firstly I should say it's a pity she didn't mix a little logic with her imagination. It is a beautiful thing to love God as she did, but it's a dangerous thing to have an illogical conception of God. The result may be anything from burning your neighbour so that his soul may be saved, to the morally cruel behaviour of this otherwise well-meaning woman . . . Yet in one sense can we blame her ? As long as it is considered blasphemous or irreverent to reason about God, what can we expect ? As a matter of fact, far from being blasphemous or irreverent, it's the best mental-spiritual exercise you can take. As soon as you are really interested in a being, whether God, angel or man, you're bound to reason about him ; it would be unnatural not

to do so. You may arrive at no definite con-
clusions perhaps, but at least you will heighten
your conception of God and not endow Him
with the undesirable attributes this woman, in
the *Garden of Allah*, endowed Him with!
But of course—and here comes the folly of it—
she was quite unconscious of the unflattering
aspersions she was casting on God. She all
too painfully realised that her husband, in her
own words, 'had insulted God,' but she little
thought that in an indirect way she herself was
insulting Him too. For one thing, to think
that a Being so great and all-loving as God
could be so small-minded and non-understanding
as to be capable of feeling insulted, is already an
insult in itself. In comparison with God, for
instance, we Initiates are as mere worms—but
even *we* aren't susceptible to insults. If a man
came into this room and said to me: 'You're an
impostor and a charlatan,' I shouldn't feel the
least inclined to give him a black eye—I so
thoroughly understand his point of view: to
such a man I *am* an impostor and a charlatan!

"But you'll say: 'What about this monk's
broken vows? What are your views with
regard to *them?*' Well, frankly I don't believe
in those sort of vows. In my opinion the taking

of vows springs from a feeling of uncertainty.
It is like tieing your own feet together when
you scent danger, in case you may be tempted
to run away. He who has completely *renounced*,
never needs to take vows, because nobody requires to bind himself to refrain from doing
what he never *wishes* to do. Somebody has
written : 'Renunciation is only true and complete when there is no *sense* of renunciation';
and that is correct. Does the adult have to
renounce the pleasures of childhood? Certainly
not ; he renounces them *inwardly* because he
has outgrown them. It's the same with adults
in wisdom—they need not take oaths that they'll
give up resentment, jealousy, envy, hatred, and
the like—they never have the temptation to
feel such emotions; they *can't* even feel them—
they've forgotten how! Or take yourselves and
your attititude to Yoga philosophy. To you it
is the background of everything. Each one of
you now knows that whatever happens you will
still be true to your philosophy. And why?
Because it's the highest interest you have in
your lives. Do you need to make vows on the
subject? Surely they would be quite super-
fluous. But supposing on the other hand you
do take a vow—say to perform a certain kind

THE TYRANNY OF VIEW-POINTS

of work, and then you lose interest in that work but continue it simply because of your vows, what sort of work will you produce as the result? Probably bad work—for what's not done with love is, with few exceptions, badly done

"And now to return to this monk. He entered that monastery when he was seventeen, knowing nothing whatever of life, yet he vowed to re-nounce life. But can anybody renounce a thing they have never known? It's a contradiction in terms. Therefore whatever vows that monk may have taken, they were not those of re-nunciation, except in mere words. If he'd been a nun, I suppose one would say he had wedded himself to God, but as God is usually considered to be of the male sex, one would need to express it differently. In any case one thing is certain: wedded or not, those broken vows would hardly break God's heart. He is not quite dependent for His happiness on the fidelity of one rather insignificant man. Just think of the unconscious conceit of that man! For that is one of the drawbacks to Dualism. Here is God who created this vast universe—probably according to that monk's conception, out of nothing—yet He's going to

worry Himself and feel insulted and pained
because one little insignificant creature living on
one of His countless earths has ceased to pray
all the day long.   It may be very flattering
to us to think that we are *necessary* to God,
but it's bad for our heads ; it tends to make
them more swollen than they are already.
The doctrine that with every trifling sin we
commit we are paining God, is perhaps a useful
one for the education of imaginative children
who can't realise the conceit it implies, but
apart from that it's a dangerous doctrine.
There is a moment in the book under dis-
cussion when the wife of this vow-breaking
monk says : 'I feel that God has been more
intent on you than on anyone I have ever
known.'   This sentence remained in my memory
on account of the boundless conceit it implies.
We laugh at a savage's conception of God as
the angry thunderer who needs propitiating,
but the savage is at least modest ; he thinks
his God a mighty God, and himself a worm—
for remember you only entertain the propitia-
tion idea if you regard someone as mightier
than yourself.

"That woman in the *Garden of Allah* thought
she believed in a mighty and a loving God,

but even so she seems to have taken it as a matter of course when He apparently prompted *her* to behave in a very *un*loving manner.   It's as if He had said : ' *My* business is love— yes—but you—you are different, *your* business is to show yourself hard and cruel, in that way you'll carry out My plans and decrees.   By your behaviour you must *force* this erring monk to return to me.   I need him more than you do.   It's true you have only the few pleasures and joys of your little world and I've the whole infinite universe for My play-ground, still—I *must* have that man.   I'm sorry to take him away from you, of course, but then you shouldn't have been so foolish as to become attached to a man like that.   The mischief's done now, so you'll just have to bear it.   In any case you've always got my love to console you, and after all it's much better than any man's. And now I'm afraid that's the best I can do for you . . .' "

   " These sentiments sound very elevated from the lips of the All-loving !   If that woman were here and I told her what I have just told you, she'd think me a blasphemer.   But it is not I who am putting those words into God's mouth, it is so to say she herself.   It's her own view-point which is responsible, not my view-point. *I'm* not blaspheming, because I don't believe such a God exists. We can't be irreverent towards a myth. And here we come to another factor in the argument—the supposition is that if a person is capable of love, he must inevitably be capable of suffering, and as this is the case with ordinary humans, it must hence be the case with God. Our monk and his pious wife imagined that God loved them so deeply that He suffered through the former's infidelity. But does this argument hold water? The one sun shines in the sky but is reflected in millions of little dew-drops; if the dew-drop is big, the reflection is big, if small, the reflection is small; if tarnished with dust, the reflection is tarnished—yet the real sun shines pure and unaffected in all its glory. Now if you imagine that sun is the unconditional feeling of Love and Bliss in Itself which it pours out over everything and everybody, can the behaviour of the individuals it shines upon alter its Love and Bliss? Certainly not; but only the more evolved can realise this, the less evolved are unable to conceive that even God—to put it crudely—'can do anything for nothing.' These latter

can't imagine the sensation of absolute Love
in itself. Their idea is that in order to love,
you must have some particular person or persons towards whom to direct that love. It's
the same with joy—there must be something
about which to feel joyous ; remove that something and the joy disappears. What was this
monk really thinking in his heart? Why, that
God was partly dependent on him for happiness, and that as soon as he misbehaved himself, God was distressed about it—so much so
that He must endeavour to retrieve him at
whatever cost. It's like an unevolved husband
feels towards his wife ; as long as she behaves
herself, he takes her as a matter of course,
but as soon as she starts to flirt with other
men, she suddenly begins to loom very important in his eyes—and in a painful way.
As I told you, that woman in the story said :
' I feel that God has been more intent on you
than on anyone I have ever known.' And here
in this sentence speaks the very human conception of the Almighty. ' Now that you've
ceased to love God, His vanity is hurt, and
hence He wants you all the more, just as the
husband wants his unfaithful wife.' Yet does
all this coincide with logic and experience ; is

there an unconditional Love, an unconditional Bliss, or not? We gurus know there is, because we've experienced that Love and Bliss in ourselves. We were taught how to experience it, and now we are trying to teach others to do likewise.

"But first we must make war against the many false conceptions of God, and all they involve. If people think of God as a jealous God they'll imagine *they* have a right to be jealous. If they think of Him as a sad God they themselves will think they can give way to sorrow; that is where the tyranny of their view-point will come in. It was because this woman in the *Garden of Allah* thought her God capable of sadness that she resigned herself to sadness and treated her husband so harshly and inhumanly in the process. Unconsciously she thought herself stronger and more heroic than God. Nobody would go and wreck her own life for a Being she knew to be incapable of feeling sorrow. The strong don't need to sacrifice themselves for the equally strong or more strong, they sacrifice themselves for the weak. That is why I say this woman subconsciously imagined herself stronger than God. And the result was Tragedy. Ah— Epictetus was very wise when he said: ' It's

not things but our *opinions* about things that
matter.' Sum up the net results of the opinions
of these two characters in the book. Because
of his opinions, this man became a monk; because of his opinions he took vows which, with
his temperament, he never should have taken;
because of his opinions he was plunged into
misery when he broke those vows; because of
his opinions he married a certain woman—people
don't marry unless they *believe* in marriage; because of his opinions he leaves her to loneliness
and sorrow, and incidentally to the bringing up
of a 'fatherless' son—for after all a father who
is shut up for life in a monastery is as good as
dead. And what of hers? Because of her
opinions she marries a man of whom she knows
practically nothing. Because of her opinions
she is all but driven to despair when she hears
he has broken his vows. Because of her opinions
she immediately moves into another tent. Because of her opinions she behaves in a hard and
inhuman way. Because of her opinions she
forces him to leave her and go back whence he
came. Because of her opinions she refuses to
tell him that she is pregnant. Because of her
opinions she can never marry again, since even
to seek for an annulment of marriage would go

contrary to her opinions. And now after all this," the Master smiled quizzically, " I hope you realise the tyranny of view-points, and how dangerous they can be. If only people would learn to *think* before they evolve their point of view, or having evolved one, would at least weigh every pro and con to see whether there are not follies and inconsistencies which need altering and readjusting ! But unfortunately most people never think out a point of view for themselves, they just adopt any one that happens to be floating around. If they admire some person in particular they'll adopt *his* view-point, quite irrespective of its suitability to their own temperament or mentality. It is on account of this diversity of human temperaments that the Great Sages who gave to the world the Yoga Philosophy divided it into several Paths—so that each student should follow that one most suited to him. Are you here in this circle all treading exactly the same path ? No, of course you're not ; how were that possible when exactly the same phase of Yoga does not appeal to all of you alike ?

"But that is somewhat by the way. The lesson I want to impress upon you to-night is this : if one species of view-point can produce unhappi-

ness and cruelty, another species can produce
the opposite.   Therefore what you who are, I
hope, learning a little wisdom must do, is to
teach people to form love-and-happiness-produc-
ing view-points, not the reverse, as did this
woman in the *Garden of Allah.*   And now in
conclusion," the Master said genially, " I think
we owe Mr. Robert Hichens a debt of gratitude
for all the food for reflection he has given us
through his book this evening.   It's true that
as he's not present it's no use expressing ourselves in the usual way—however——

" Are there any questions ? "

" I don't quite understand your attitude to
those broken vows," said Wilson tentatively,
" you seem to have made rather light of them.
Surely vows once made ought to be kept ? "

M.H. smiled to himself.   " Firstly," he answered, " I was looking at the matter from
God's point of view ; secondly, whether vows
ought to be kept entirely depends on circumstances.   If you credit God with even a degree
of knowledge and foresight He must have
known in advance that the monk in question
might possibly *not* keep those vows, therefore
why should He be upset when what He fore-
saw happened ?   As to whether vows should be

kept or broken—that depends on the underlying reason. A man who breaks a vow through weakness may be forgiven but not exactly admired. On the other hand the man who breaks a vow because he has come to alter his convictions since the time it was made is worthy of admiration. It is *motive* that counts. If you injure others when you break a vow then you must not break it."

Clare said : " You spoke of Love in Itself— the sensation of Love without an object ; but I've read in books on theosophy that even God divided Himself into many so as to have an object or rather a multitude of objects to love. I don't quite understand how the two state-ments agree."

" Supposing you were the first person in the world to discover gold and you wanted other people to profit by that gold—could you ever entertain such a thought unless you had the gold to begin with and felt the sensation of benevolence in your own heart? Similarly God already had the 'sensation' of Love, but He wanted others to profit by that Love. That, I think, is more or less the idea expressed in the books. Any more questions ? "

One of the men students asked : " Do you

think that monk ought to have gone back to his monastery or stayed with his wife?"

" I should have thought, my son, that you could answer that question yourself," the Master said, "perhaps one of the other *chelas* will oblige."

Mr. Galais volunteered : " If his convictions told him it was the right thing to do, it *was* right for *him*."

" Any more questions?" from the Master.

Nobody responded.

CHAPTER XXV

THE DYAN CHOHAN AND THE BOOK

"I WANT to write another book about you," I said to M.H. the following morning. He had asked Viola and me to come to him because he wanted to tell us of some little service of a private nature which he wished us to perform and we had just finished discussing the details of it. "Would you object if a sequel to *The Initiate* appeared?"

He laughed.

"There's a most imposing Indian Master here," said Viola, "I can see him standing behind your chair, M.H., and hear him saying: 'Yes, let him write that book, *we* wish it.'"

M.H. laughed again. "Of course if *they* want it——" he broke off with a gesture.

"But don't you think it might do some good?" I asked, "judging from the number of letters I had about the first one?"

"Yes, I think it *might*," he admitted.

"The Indian Master—at least I suppose he must be a Master," said Viola, "he looks so perfectly glorious—is smiling and saying: 'There is no doubt that it *would* be *very* beneficial.'"

"Young lady," M.H. teased her, "those clair-voyant faculties of yours——"

But Viola's answering smile was rather grave. She told me that the Being she saw had such a very exalted and impressive atmosphere about Him.

"Who *is* it she sees?" I asked M.H., wishing I could see too.

"One who takes a special interest in *you*, my son," he said, suddenly becoming serious, "a Dyan Chohan—that must suffice for you."

"But a Dyan Chohan is even greater than a Master . . ." I stammered, feeling awed but intensely grateful for His interest in one so un-worthy as myself.

M.H. nodded. "My children, if you hadn't made up your minds to do what I asked, that Dyan Chohan would not have appeared to you here. "Is he still there, Viola?"

"Yes—I hear him say: 'My loved ones, I give you my blessing. At your marriage I will come again. Farewell,'"

There was a pause. "Now he has gone," she added reverently. We were all silent for a few moments; then I saw M.H. looking at me with one of his whimsical expressions, and I felt he knew what was in my mind: I had been wondering why he had asked Viola that last question. Surely he could see perfectly well himself whether the Dyan Chohan was still there or not. It was Viola who afterwards enlightened me.

"He always does that," she said, "he only uses his own powers when there's no pupil handy—haven't you noticed with the Yoga exercises that he never shows you them himself, but gets a pupil to show them instead? I suppose it's his modesty."

"But about this book," said M.H., breaking the silence in a cheerful and business-like tone of voice.

"Would you allow me to reconstruct some of the lectures from my notes?" I asked tentatively, "or would that be verging on the indiscreet?"

"If you *want* to include some of the talks you can save yourself a lot of trouble by simply asking Heddon to lend you his copy of them. He takes some of them down in short-hand for the library. You can easily get a few of them typed."

"That'll be splendid!"

"The only thing is, I should want to have a say in the selection. Some of them are only suited for initiates and not for the general public. We'll go through them together one day before you leave."

CHAPTER XXVI

MUSIC AND "MIRACLES"

ON New Year's Eve M.H. had invited all his pupils to dinner, and afterwards there was music, also reciting, and "stunts" of various kinds. One of the *Chelas* played a few modern piano works, Debussy's, Ravel's, and others. Some songs were sung by a really excellent singer. Viola read one or two passages out of her mystic books, I "intoned" some of my poems, and Arkwright gave us three or four character-sketches. He proved himself a comedian of the first rank, and the audience was in fits of laughter. The most enthralling part of the evening, however, was the half-hour in which the Master was prevailed upon to show us a few phenomena. He preluded his performance by reminding us that what we were about to witness was all *Maya*. He also said : "Some occult societies, the Theosophical, for instance, think it's *infra dig.* to produce phenomena of any sort—but the truth is, since Madame Blavatsky has moved on to another plane, there's nobody in the Society who *can* produce them. Besides which motive is everything. If I show you a few things to-night it's to amuse you, I grant, but it's also to give you more faith. You may ask why, for the same reason, I don't take the big hall here and give an exhibition? The answer is, I should not increase the faith of the general public if I *did*—their faith and yours are two different things—they would merely explain everything away by calling my performances conjuring-tricks. *You* wouldn't. Wasn't old Madame Blavatsky 'proved' an imposter in spite of everything?"

" How about doing some of *her* stunts?" suggested Arkwright.

" Which, for instance?"

"Wasn't there something with a table—fixing the thing so that no one could budge it?"

M.H. smiled. "Anybody want to try and move that little table over there?" he said, pointing to the back of the room.

Several of the pupils, including myself, went over to it, pushed and pulled and tried to lift it

with all our strength, while the rest looked on
and laughed at our efforts—but it was as firm as
a rock ; we could not move it one fraction of an
inch.   At last we gave it up as hopeless.

"Try now," said M.H., amused.

Arkwright took hold of it and lifted it with
one hand . . .

"Any more suggestions?" M.H. asked.

"Would you not make yourself invisible?"
said one of the students—an Irish-American.

"All right, but first watch me blow rings."
He took a long puff at his cigar, and a moment
afterwards two perfect rings on which we all
fixed our eyes with admiration slowly ascended.
The next instant when I came to look at M.H.
he had vanished—the chair on the platform was
empty.

"My!" said Clare, who was sitting next to
me ; and that one interjection was more than
expressive.

Suddenly we heard the chord of C Major on
the piano.   All eyes were at once turned in that
direction, but only to find that no one was anywhere near the instrument.

"Spooks!" came Master's voice, and there
he was once more seated in his chair and beam-
ing at us.   "What's the next suggestion?"

" Would it be possible to—how shall I put it —*duplicate* yourself ? " I asked.

" Well—exactly how ? "

" Suppose you remain in that chair—then we'll open the folding doors at the back there, and you'll materialise a duplicate of yourself in that room ? "

" I see you're possessed of some imagination, my friend," he said with a twinkle, " but I'm an accomodating person, so you shall have your wish. In one minute from now somebody can open the doors."

He sat bolt upright in the chair and closed his eyes. Arkwright pulled out his watch. There was silence. " The minute is up," he said finally, " open the doors."

We all looked towards the ante-room and there was the exact replica of M.H., including the chair and platform. The effect was so amazing that I found it very difficult to believe my senses, and kept looking from the one M.H. to the other. All of a sudden a bell rang ; it had a most beautiful tone, and seemed to come from the ceiling. Everybody looked up, but there was nothing to be seen.

" More spooks," smiled M. H. and relit his cigar. His duplicate had disappeared. "What's the next to be ? " he asked.

" Levitation," somebody suggested.

"Oh, Arkwright can do that—come along, my boy."

Arkwright went up to the platform, and between them they lifted the chair on to the floor.

" Now then, full length on your back and keep rigid."

Arkwright did as he was told; the Master stood over him, placed one hand about two feet above his recumbent body, then slowly raised it and Arkwright rose in the air, as if he were being pulled up by an invisible cord. He remained for about one minute suspended a yard above the top of the platform, then slowly sank down again.

A burst of applause greeted this performance, and Arkwright got up and made a mock bow.

" Have you had enough ? " M. H. asked.

There were cries of " No, no, please show us some more ! "

" Well, then, out with your suggestions ! "

" Let's have the musical-box stunt," from Heddon.

M. H. went to a desk, opened a drawer, and took out one of those little musical boxes that are played by turning a handle.

" Now who wants to lock the doors and put

the keys in their pocket to show there's no deception?" he enquired.

Mr. Galais volunteered. Having locked the doors he held up the keys for us to see, and then dropped them into his pocket.

"This phenomenon," said M. H. "is something the spiritists produce. *We* require no spirits of the departed. Are we ready? Well, then—go!"

The musical box ascended in the air, revolved several times round the room over our heads, then disappeared right through one of the closed doors, and we heard it still playing in the passage. There was a thud—it had evidently fallen down—and silence. Some of the company looked dumbfounded, others merely amused—the latter had witnessed this phenomenon before.

"Better make certain the musical box *is* outside," said M. H., with the suspicion of a wink. "Galais—forward with the keys."

Mr. Galais produced them from his pocket, held them up on view, and proceeded to unlock the doors. Many of us crowded round him; and sure enough, there outside on the mat was the little toy. Mr. Galais picked it up and handed it to M. H. who put it back in his desk.

"One more," he said then, "what's it to be?"

"My mother sent me a large bunch of grapes," said a pianist named Hausmann, "it's lying in my dining-room at home on the buffet—can you transport it here?"

"Somebody fetch me a newspaper," was Master's reply. Arkwright went out of the room and presently appeared with a copy of the *New York Herald*. M. H. made it into a cone-shaped receptacle, closed his eyes for a few moments, then delved down with his hand into the cone, and produced a magnificent bunch of muscatels.

"Are the company allowed to taste them?" he asked Hausmann genially.

"Sure—I move they be handed round."

We all tasted them, and they were genuine grapes right enough, unusually luscious ones, in fact.

"Well," said M. H. finally, "I think we've had enough miracles now. I suggest that Hausmann should play us a little Scriabine."

"And then that you give us a little talk," somebody added, "it'll be a good way of beginning the New Year—for us!"

The others chimed in with: "Yes, do—please!"

M. H. smiled. "Well, as you wish . . ."

"Since we are concerned," he began, after the Scriabine was over, "with anniversaries to-night, a few thoughts on the subject present themselves. One is that to keep an annivesary which has sorrowful associations is a waste of good emotion, and therefore unwise and quite useless. It is bad enough as it is to dwell on pain when we can't help ourselves, but actually to force ourselves to dwell on it for one particular day in the year is really very foolish. Religious festivals have their esoteric significance—Christmas, for one,—but that is another matter. Christmas inspires people to feel joy, which is a *con*structive emotion, but a death-anniversary moves them to feel sadness and selfishness which are *de*structive emotions. As to New Year's Eve—there are many who will no doubt look sorrowfully back and think : 'In this now expiring year I lost such and such a friend or relative'; while there are others and wiser ones who will think not : 'How sad I have been the last twelve months,' but : 'How much progress have I made in my evolution? How much nearer am I to my ideal?' And perhaps to encourage themselves they will conjure up in their minds all the joys and beauties of that Ideal, and picture themselves as having attained it, with all the felicity inherent in that attainment. And that would be a wise and fruitful way of seeing the old year out. You will have noticed, perhaps, that when you've become inspired by some book to adopt a certain course in your lives, and then have grown a little luke-warm, and lost some of your interest, if you re-read the book it inspires you anew, and once again with fresh energy you forge ahead. And so I thought that to-night, while the old year is passing away, I would like to take the place of that book and try to bring your thoughts to bear on the joys and beauties of that particular Ideal all of you here so ardently wish to attain. For although it is my policy to keep that Ideal always before your mind, to-night I will dwell on the almost unimaginable advantages of having attained it—that by my so doing you may perhaps strive with renewed energy *to* attain it; and of course by *it*, I mean Love as a permanent consciousness, and Bliss as a permanent consciousness.

" In one of the ancient Indian scriptures there is a very apt fable. It relates how a man, who complained that the earth we walk on is all rough and covered with stones and thorns, hit on what he thought was a wonderful discovery.

He said : ' Let us collect all the leather in the
world and cover the whole of the earth's surface
with it, then everywhere we walk will be lovely
and smooth, and there'll be no more sore feet.'
A little child was present at the time and heard
what he said, but being more imaginative than
the man put forward a much better suggestion.
' It's going to be a terrible lot of trouble,' the
child said, 'to cover the whole earth with leather,
so why not just tie a bit of leather on to your
feet instead; the effect will be exactly the same.'
And it is just this effect you are aiming at when,
instead of trying to alter the external world in
order to adjust it to your own desires, you strive
to alter your own consciousness instead. It is
true you may endeavour to do a bit of good here
and there, but what you actually achieve is, when
all is said, but very little. It is almost like trying to empty a pond by means of a spoon.
Still, we must not forget that if a thousand or
ten thousand people were to start ladling out
that pond with even so small an implement, an
appreciable effect would be produced. But—to
carry my simile further—who would wish to do
something so monotonous and fatiguing unless
they were possessed of an internal joy which no
task, however arid and strenuous, could take

from them ? And it's the same with the task of trying to do good in the world. As long as we have not attained Love and Joy as permanent states of consciousness, our capacity to do good will be limited by our *desire* to do good— at least very largely so. Do you not wish to help those you love more than those you do not love? Most certainly you do. Therefore think what it would mean if you could love everybody —not because all persons in the world are so attractive and lovable that they awaken your love, but because an ever-present consciousness of Love exists within yourselves and, like the sun, rays out in all directions on the 'just and unjust' alike.

"Now, there are some people who can't get rid of the notion that spiritual Love for all humanity is something rather too remote or abstract or cold or dull to be worth such a lot of striving for ; they want something more concrete, more emotional, like the love between lovers or intensely devoted friends. These people, in fact, are confounding benevolence or a mere feeling of kindliness, with love. I am not saying that benevolence isn't a beautiful thing as far as it goes, but it is a very mild emotion indeed compared with Love-Consciousness ; even the affection between friends is mild compared with *that*. For remember, the most devoted of friends are not thinking of one another *all* the time. You may get a thrill of affection whenever you *do* think of a being you love very much, but just because your thoughts are not centred on that being the *whole* of the day those thrills are comparatively rare, so cannot be termed part of your normal consciousness. Besides which, if you have to separate from your friend, either you suffer, or else--should that separation last a long time—your love begins to grow dim, for *conditional* love is largely dependent for its existence on memory. How could anybody ever love an absent one unless he were possessed of a memory —would it not be an impossibility? So you see that when people try to compare unfavourably conditional personal love with unconditional spiritual Love, they do so because they have never experienced the latter and therefore do not *know*. Let them once experience it, even for the space of one minute, and for ever after they will talk differently. It is *not* something abstract and luke-warm and coolly detached—it is joy and peace and warmth and beauty all blended into one. There was once a yonth who smelt a strange and beautiful perfume, and could not account for it at all.   He put his nose into every flower he saw thinking it might come from one or the other, but none of the flowers exhaled a scent that was anything like it in the least. Then finally he discovered the truth : the perfume was on himself, and it was he who was carrying it wherever he went ; for the previous day his beloved had dropped one drop of some sweet-smelling essential oil on to his turban, but the circumstance had escaped his memory.   And just as it was with that young man so it is with those who have attained Love-Consciousness— they too carry that Love and Joy around with them wherever they go, for it is with*in* them-selves instead of with*out*.   Enter where they may they find an atmosphere of Love, because it is they who bring that atmosphere ; and because Love beautifies everything, even sordid and ugly places seem beautiful to *them*.   Think, for example, when you take a railway-journey and you come to a crowded station where a lot of people want to get into your carriage.   Per-haps among them there is a not over-clean woman with a baby, so that you say to yourself : ' I only hope *she* won't get in here with her baby that'll cry and make a horrid noise, disturbing my reflections.'   And then perhaps she and her

baby do get into the carriage and you feel uncomfortable and disgusted and move as far away
from her as you possibly can. Well, are you
feeling happy in your discomfort and disgust?
You are only hoping she'll get out at the next
station and rid you of her disagreeable presence.
But how very different it would all be if, because
of a never-to-be-banished feeling of love within
yourself, you loved even that woman and her
baby, and were glad she should enter your
carriage. What would it matter to you if you
weren't able to continue your reflections or the
reading of your book or paper? You would be
just as happy sitting doing nothing as enjoying
the most exciting novel. For your happiness
would not depend for its existence on a book or
on whether you were in a stuffy railway carriage
or on a mountain-top. You would be happy
anywhere, because you yourself would be *one*
with Happiness, as the really healthy man may
be said to be one with health.

"And now on your efforts this New Year, I
give you my blessings and wishes that you may
all come nearer to the Goal. Learn more and
more to use your God-given imaginations to that
end ; learn more and more to *think* Love and to
think Joy, that you may become what potentially

you are—the Eternal Ineffable Self—the Ab-
solute-Existence-Knowledge-Love-and-Bliss."

The Master's speech had been a short one,
but it had been unusually impressive, especially
its conclusion. The wonderful love in his voice
as he gave us his blessing, I will not attempt
to describe. I can only say that its power
and beauty moved every one of us. For quite
a minute after he had finished, although there
was a general movement towards leave-taking,
none of us spoke ; and when finally we did,
it was in an undertone.

I was wondering whether I should go up
to M.H. and say good night when Mr. Galais,
as the eldest of the *chelas*, got up on to the
platform and said a few words of thanks to
the Master in the name of all present. It was
not only for the enjoyable and varied evening
he thanked, but for everything Master had
done for us in the past, and he knew would
do in the future. He said he realised that
anything he might say could not express even
an infinitesimal part of the gratitude we all felt,
but there were times when he was unable to
refrain from at least making the attempt—such
as it was.

When he had finished, M.H. in return thanked

him and all of us for *our* thanks, and said that
in addition he wished to express his indebted-
ness to those who had played and sung and
recited that evening, and so added to the
general enjoyment.   After which with a smile
he wished us all a happy New Year.

EPILOGUE

IN writing this Epilogue I feel like the old-fashioned novelist who always thought it necessary to round off his characters. The difference is that whereas he probably wrote his final chapter immediately after he had written the foregoing ones, I am writing my final chapter after a lapse of several years.

Viola and I have now been married for some time, and the child which M. H. desired we should have, is fast growing into a sturdy boy. Although he appears to possess an unusually happy nature, he does not express that happiness in the "musical" way I once feared he might. He has neither been given nor asked for a tin trumpet on which to toot discordantly while his father is trying to work . . .

Shortly before his birth, our Master told us who he was, or rather, who he had been, and as I think and hope only one or two very close friends know who *we* are, when denuded of our pseudonyms, I may say that not only were we greatly astonished but felt even more greatly honoured. In fact we have many times during the last few years had reason to be thankful we carried out Master's wishes. Not that things were easy at first : they were extremely difficult ; but the difficult time passed quickly and is now almost forgotten.

Although I have not seen M.H. in the flesh since leaving Boston, he occasionally—when he thinks we need him—visits us in his "Astral," and as Viola can see him clairvoyantly and clairaudiently hear all he says, she repeats his messages to me. There is another mode of communication which he sometimes adopts, and through which he is able to speak to me directly, and I to him, but of this I am not at liberty to write. That he is often with me when I am busy upon some inspirational work I know— again through Viola—who has on several occasions sensed his presence. She tells me that I, who have only seen him in the flesh, can form no idea of what he really looks like. Though in the physical he has a noble and arresting face, in his "Astral Form" she says his beauty is not to be described. His aura is so large that it extends far beyond the house whenever he visits us.   Even *his* visits are not entirely without their humorous side, for there are times when our cook, who is somewhat clairvoyant without realising it, wonders why everything in the kitchen "looks pink," and whether there may not be something wrong with her eyes!   We, of course, cannot very well enlighten her . . .

M.H. never writes to me, which might seem curious because I know through Heddon, his secretary, that he *does* dictate a great many letters; but as he can communicate by other means, this is not a matter for surprise.   But I do receive indirect news of him and his doings through Arkwright, who corresponds with me. One of his letters contained some startling news about Clare.

Our parting had not been quite so painful as I had anticipated, for she and her mother had intended "making the trip" to England the following summer.   But I never saw Clare again—she died of pneumonia three months after I left the United States.   "She passed out in Canada, and quite painlessly," Arkwright wrote.   For several days she had been unconscious, and only regained consciousness an hour or so before she died.   Master was with her at the last—this she herself told Viola who sees her from time to time when she visits us from the "Other Side." Like many people on the point of death, Clare had become clairvoyant for a while, and had seen Master standing beside her to comfort her and lead her across the border. She is very happy and very helpful to us in many ways, for she describes the conditions on her plane, and we have learnt a number of interesting details from her. Now of course I understand why Master would not tell her the future in relation to herself and me. Nevertheless her death puzzled me—more than it distressed me—and I had to appeal to him for enlightenment.

"Why should you take a pupil," I asked, "when you must have known that she would die a few months afterwards? It seems sheer waste of time."

He smiled his characteristic gentle smile. "My son," he replied, "I took her partly as a greater test for *you*, and partly —well—it's not necessary for you to know the other reason. It would have been comparatively easy for you to grow fond of Viola if you had not been in love with Clare. Yet even apart from that, there was no waste: do you suppose that just because

Clare is what the ignorant call dead, she is parted from me and can no longer be my *chela* ? "

I laughed at my own foolishness.

"And so," I said afterwards to Viola, "it's a good job I never married Clare—I'd have been a widower by now."

"And it's a good job I never married Norman," she replied, "or I should have been perfectly wretched all the time. As it is, we're both of us happy together, and we both have a spiritual consciousness which has been mighty cheap at the price."

"And have still retained our sense of humour," I added with mischievous irony. "Marvellous, isn't it ? "